STEVEN SPIELBERG PRESENTS
A MATTHEW ROBBINS FILM

*batteries not included

"BATTERIES NOT INCLUDED"

HUME CRONYN • JESSICA TANDY

Screenplay by BRAD BIRD & MATTHEW ROBBINS and
BRENT MADDOCK & S.S. WILSON

Story by MICK GARRIS Music by JAMES HORNER

Executive Producers STEVEN SPIELBERG KATHLEEN KENNEDY
FRANK MARSHALL

Produced by RONALD L. SCHWARY Directed by MATTHEW ROBBINS

AMBLIN
ENTERTAINMENT

A UNIVERSAL Picture

Meyer

*batteries not included

A novel by Wayland Drew
Based on a screenplay by Brad Bird & Matthew Robbins
and Brent Maddock & S.S. Wilson   Story by Mick Garris

BERKLEY BOOKS, NEW YORK

BATTERIES NOT INCLUDED

A Berkley Book / published by arrangement with
MCA Publishing Rights, a Division of MCA, Inc.

PRINTING HISTORY
Berkley edition / December 1987

ISBN: 0-425-10105-3

A BERKLEY BOOK® TM 757,375
Berkley Books are published by The Berkley Publishing Group,
200 Madison Avenue, New York, New York 10016.
The name "BERKLEY" and the "B" logo
are trademarks belonging to Berkley Publishing Corporation.

PRINTED IN THE UNITED STATES OF AMERICA

10 9 8 7 6 5 4 3 2 1

*batteries
not included

_____

IMAGINE PASSING OVER New York on a clear afternoon. Imagine seeing, in the Lower East Side, an area of devastation apparently no different from many others where the city is changing itself, demolishing buildings from other times and replacing them with glass towers. Imagine sensing something unusual about this site, dropping closer to reconnoiter, and discovering that the destruction is not quite complete. One old apartment still stands there, shocked and very vulnerable amidst the swirling dust, like a pine that has alone survived a hurricane in a forest. Most of its windows stare blankly out at the surrounding rubble, but a few have curtains. Incredibly, this building is inhabited . . .

From the several hats spread on her bed, Faye Riley chose the one Frank had given her in 1942.

They were young then and in love for the first time. It had

been Easter when he bought it. He had a 72-hour leave before his carrier sailed, and he had looked so handsome in his whites. Those bell-bottoms! That hat! She had taken the whole weekend off work so they could be together, and she had never been happier. She remembered it that way— happy. But she also remembered crying that weekend, ter- rified that the ship would be torpedoed and she would never see Frank again. "I'll come back," he said. "I prom- ise. I'll come *back!*"

He had bought her the hat to make her smile again. He had laughed at first when she picked it out. "It looks like a bowl on a plate, upside down." But when she put it on, he had stopped laughing. "Beautiful!" he said.

When the ship sailed, she had stood with other wives and sweethearts on the pier, biting her lip and trying to smile while she peered up into the sun above the camou- flaged hull, far up to the superstructure where she believed she saw her Frank, a tiny, vulnerable human speck, wav- ing.

He had come back, just as he said he would. They got married right away, and they had Bobby, and all these wonderful years together, with the cafe and all their friends.

"How many years?" A wrinkled and white-haired old woman spoke up from across the room, and Faye Riley had to wave and make a face to be certain she was looking into a mirror.

"Forty," she said. "No, forty-five. No . . ." She couldn't remember exactly. It didn't matter anyway. What mattered was that they had been happy years. *"Happy,"* she said firmly, and the woman in the mirror smiled and nodded, yes.

Faye fixed the hat on her white hair and tied its ribbons under her wrinkled chin. It was still a beautiful hat. The mauve flowers had faded a bit and the wide brim was grayer and dustier, but it was still a striking hat. People stared when she wore it. Of course, people often stared at her no matter what outfit she was wearing. She would smile at them with grave dignity. Sometimes, young men cupped their hands and called at her from across the street, and she would nod to them even if she did not hear what they said, even if she did not recognize them as any of Bobby's friends.

She put on her pink bathrobe over her underclothes, found her shopping cart in the closet, and crept down the stairs and along the hall to the door, carrying her shoes. She could hear Frank talking to Sid Hogenson in the cafe farther down the hall, but she did not want them to hear her. They would stop her. They would call Muriel. Muriel Hogenson would take her by the arm and lead her back upstairs, saying it was time for her nap. Muriel would give her another of those wretched pills that always made her feel so tired. *Senility,* the doctors had said. *Aggravated by shock.* Faye grunted. What did they know!

Quietly she unbolted the door and tiptoed through the vestibule with her eyes shut tight. Smiling, full of anticipation, she opened the front door.

What would it be today?

Would it be 1925? Sometimes it was. Some days, East Ninth Street was exactly as it had been in her childhood, slow and colorful in the summer sun. Large-bellied men called to one another from the doorways of the shops. Aproned women laughed. Delivery boys swept past on bicycles. In those days, awnings adorned the street, and Faye would skip through their shade down to Majursky's to pick a two-cent licorice-pipe out of a tall glass jar. There were still cart horses then, and sometimes she would take sugar cubes from the bowls on the cafe tables and hold them out, flat-palmed, for the beasts to snuffle up with their velvet lips. In those days the street was alive with cheerful sparrows, drawn to the seeds in the horse droppings, and robins still tugged worms out of backyard grass. Sometimes, on her roller skates, Faye would glide around the end of a dripping ice wagon and find a blue-green splinter of ice, while the iceman carried blocks with his tongs and his horse whinnied to others pulling bread wagons, milk wagons, wagons heaped with scrap iron and rags. Sometimes in winter the street would be so slick with hard-packed snow that she and her friends could catch the tail of a passing wagon and skid along for blocks, holding on to one another like the laughing tail of a kite.

Some days when she escaped from Frank and the Hogensons, the street was like that. She would meet old friends she hadn't seen for decades, and she would run with them and skip, and play hopscotch just as if they were all eleven.

But what about today? What would East Ninth Street be like today?

Faye opened her eyes.

Ah! How wonderful! It was 1948, another favorite time! What a feeling there had been, then, with the war over and the boys back home, settling down. The street was a community then, one big family, and people helped each other as they do in families, without even thinking. If there was something you could do, you did it, and later the favor was always repaid in wonderful, magical ways.

At least, that was how Faye remembered it.

Her baby carriage waited at the bottom of the stairs.

Carefully she carried Bobby down and tucked him in. Then she was off, a young matron, to do the marketing.

Behind her, music and laughter drifted out under the awnings of the cafe. In 1948, Rileys' Cafe was always full of people coming and going, talking and joking. Flirting. The neon Wurlitzer was always playing one of the Dorseys, or Artie Shaw, or Woody Herman, or a Glenn Miller tune that had meant so much during the war.

Some days after breakfast, or after lunch when most people had gone back to work, she and Frank would drop some nickels into the machine, watch the mechanical arms pick out the records, and then dance the slow dances in the little cleared space in the center of the cafe. They would dance cheek-to-cheek, and she would not have to stretch up on her toes, because Frank was short. Later there would be lots of other people dancing with them, but in the afternoons they would be all alone, with the world going past outside.

In the evening, other couples would come to Rileys', many other couples, and the residents of 817 East Ninth Street would come down to join them, and Marty Schwartz was always ready with his Graflex and flashbulbs to take pictures of smiling groups in the booths while the music played and played.

Such days!

Ecstatic, quite oblivious to reality, Faye Riley passed down East Ninth Street through a summer morning in 1948, proudly pushing the baby carriage with her infant son. All the way to the corner she waved to friends and neighbors, acknowledging with a graceful inclination of her head the gentlemen who raised hats to her, stopping frequently to allow the women to admire her fine son. How beautiful it all was! How full of promise!

She swept past the pharmacy on the corner of Avenue D

and on towards Majursky's Market in midblock. Here
again she stopped often to chat with friends, and here again
she was overwhelmed with the soft beauty of it all—like a
vision. Like a dream.

Only when she reached the place where Majursky's
had once been did reality descend on her. Only then,
when the shopping cart she was pushing bumped over
some loose bricks and hit what was left of the concrete
step did the soft visions of the past fade and the grim
present replace them.

Majursky's was gone.

All that remained was the roofless shell of the building,
with men in hard hats swarming over it, swinging wrecking
bars. Where her old friends, Walt and Moira, had stood
smiling so many years behind their counter, ready to help
her, clouds of dust swirled, and wires dangled from shattered plaster.

Confused, Faye Riley stared at what was left of the
building. She hated reality. She hated it when Frank led her
to the cracked and grimy old window of Rileys' Cafe, and
pointing to the devastation outside, said, "There it is, kid.
That's today. That's reality."

Now here it was, surrounding her, and she was all
alone. Horrible!

Nothing was left of what she used to know. The old
neighborhood was gone. Flattened. The cheerful little
shops had vanished. The elegant apartments lay in ruins.
Sidewalks where she had skipped and rolled her hoop so
many years before were now cracked and heaved, strewn
with rubble, clogged with mud from bulldozers. The folks
from her girlhood were all gone.

"Gone where?" she asked aloud, stopping suddenly.
"They must still be *somewhere*."

But in their place were strangers indifferent to her,

sweeping through this blighted place in closed cars, or grumbling along in trucks that hissed like fierce cats when they stopped at corners, or lurched across sidewalks. What was going on? Who *were* these people? Who was this old man washing in a dribble of water from a hydrant, straightening up to stare at her openmouthed?

Who were those young men calling to her across the street, and that one with the moustache and the sleek hair, his hands to his mouth shouting, "Hey, Grandma, you need some help? You come see Carlos, eh? Come see the Crusaders. We help old ladies get where they gotta go."

Why were they *laughing*?

Frightened now, Faye backed into the street, staring wildly around at what was left of the neighborhood. Rubble, that was what was left. Mounds of rubble, and trucks, and bulldozers, and a gang of workmen, with a crane in the midst of the devastation, erecting a huge sign with a picture of gleaming apartment towers: LACEY PLAZA—ELEGANCE, CONVENIENCE, SECURITY.

A truck rumbled towards her, its air horn growling, and she hurried back onto the sidewalk, staring at the sign and its looming vision of the future. Beyond the sign, across two blocks of rubble, stood the little old four-storey apartment building with Rileys' Cafe on the ground floor. Bulldozers prowled around it like big cats, ready to pounce.

"Bobby?" Faye said. "Where are you?" She was quite lost in this new world, without bearings or certainties except that building: home.

Frantically she scrambled straight towards it around and over the heaps of rubble. Workmen shouted at her, but she paid no attention. Machines snarled around her, but she ignored them. Her empty shopping cart bounced along behind her. Her pink hat with the mauve flowers got knocked askew. She scraped her foot on the edge of a brick. "Bobby," she said, beginning to cry the dry and silent crying of a forlorn old lady. "Oh, Bobby!"

At a corner table in the cafe, Frank Riley took off his glasses and brushed tears of laughter out of his eyes with a large checkered handkerchief. "Terrible, Sid! Terrible! 'I remember your mane perfectly, I just can't recall the pace.' What a line! Listen, it reminds me of the one about the guy who's way out in the country painting a church. Stop me if you've heard it. Guy almost gets finished and he runs low on paint."

"Yeah?" Sid Hogenson leaned on the table, grinning, working a toothpick in the corner of his mouth.

"'Damn it!' fella says. 'Now what am I gonna do? Too late to get more paint and only half a wall to go.' Suddenly, an idea!"

"Yeah. Yeah."

"Fella thinks to himself, 'Hey, this is *latex* paint, right. Water-base. All I gotta do is water it down a bit. Spread it out.' Get the picture, Sid?"

"Yeah."

"So he does that. Finishes the job, and he's just walking around admiring it when the biggest, goddammedest thunderstorm you ever seen opens up right overhead. Pow! Bam! And when the rain stops, paint's gone. Washed clean off."

"Yeah?"

"Every square inch! Poor guy claps his hands to his head. Says 'Good God, *now* what am I gonna do?' Big voice comes outta heaven. Says, 'Repaint, repaint, and thin no more!'"

"Awww," Sid Hogenson howled. "Terrible! Terrible! 'Thin no more.'" He swatted the table so hard the empty coffee cups bounced on their saucers. "Listen, that reminds me of the one about the guys paintin' the ceiling of a church. Big scaffolds, see. Stop me if you've heard it. Down below..."

"Stop."

"You heard it?"

"No. I'm just gonna get us some more coffee. Hold on."

Stooped a little, squinting through his bifocals, his big apron hanging loose since he had lost so much weight, Frank Riley started towards the kitchen with the two empty cups. At that moment, a six-wheel truck, rumbling past with a massive load of broken concrete, shook the whole cafe, jiggling the plates on their glass shelves, trembling the records in the old jukebox, and jarring several photographs on the walls.

"Dammit!" Frank shouted. "Goddammit! That's the fourth time today!" He set the cups down and shook a scrawny fist towards the receding truck. "What're you tryin' to do, knock the place down while we're still here? Go ahead! That's what you'll have to do anyway!" He went over to straighten the photos. Old friends smiled at him out of dusty frames. There was Cy George the night he won the bowling trophy, and there was Emma Kowalski with all her friends the day she got her first bit part in the movies, and there he was himself, twenty-five years ago, working at the grill in his cook's tall hat. And there was Faye, Faye when she was still waitressing, looking so great in that starched cap and uniform...

"She's gone!" Muriel Hogenson thumped down the hall and into the cafe on the square heels of her sensible shoes. "I knew it! I knew it, goddammit! I turn my back for twenty minutes to do a little cleaning and what happens? She escapes! She gets past you!"

Frank peered over his glasses. "Cart gone?" Muriel nodded.

"Majursky's," Sid said, getting up and hurrying after his wife, who was now headed out the front door of the cafe. "Don't worry, Frank. We'll bring her right back."

"Don't *worry!* But what if . . ."

The little brass bell tinkled as the door slammed shut.

Frank rushed after them. His heart raced. He suddenly had trouble getting breath.

Outside, pale sunlight filtered through clouds of dust. To his left, the Hogensons disappeared into the now-empty lot where the twin building to 817 had stood until three weeks before. To his right, East Ninth Street stretched away past other buildings in various stages of demolition, empty of pedestrians. Across the street, to the south, the vacant lots reached right through the block.

Frank hurried up the steps of the apartment entrance next to the cafe so that he could see more clearly past the machinery, into the rubble heaps. Sure enough, close to the spot where a crane was heaving a giant sign into place, he saw a bobbing bit of pink. "Faye! Goddammit!"

He ran. He ran blindly across the street, aware only of that dot of pink that was the hat he had bought for his best girl long, long ago.

He embraced her when he got to her. He gathered her into his arms and drew her close and put his hand on the back of her white head, under the pink hat. "Faye, honey. Faye. For the love of Mike, where you been?"

"I did the marketing. Somebody's got to do the marketing."

Frank stared at the empty cart, its wheels twisted from her journey through the ruins. Gently, still gasping for breath, he led her towards home. "That's great, honey. What'd you buy?"

"Nice melons. He had nice melons today. And he sends regards, Walt Majursky. He wants to know when Bobby's next baseball game is. He wants to bring all his family. He says he's never *seen* a pitcher..."

"Faye, there hasn't been a baseball..."

But she was calling, "Bobby! Bobby!" to the driver of a bulldozer parked right in front of the cafe. CHIEF BROOM was painted in large letters across its flat back. The driver was a bulky man in a checkered shirt and faded blue nylon vest. He turned at the sound of her voice and tipped back his hard hat, grinning. "Bobby? Must be some mistake, ma'am. My name's Gus."

"You got a nerve!" Frank shouted at him.

"Hey! Just comin' in for a coffee, Pop."

"Get it someplace else. Back it up! Clear off!"

The diesel roared.

"And be *gentle!*"

"Gentle," Gus laughed as the immense cleats ground the asphalt to powder. "Sure."

Another crack opened in the bottom of the window, zig-zagging towards the faded gold lettering.

"Bobby?"

"He isn't Bobby, Faye. Just a guy with a warped sense of humor."

"Maybe he's seen Bobby."

"Uh-unh, he hasn't, honey. Come on now. Come on inside."

Grimly the old man guided his wife into the cafe and sat her down at a table near the window. His hand trembled as he poured mugs of coffee for them both.

Faye sniffed. "I don't smell bacon. Is it Sunday, Frank? Monday and Tuesday don't smell at all because Cream of

Wheat is instant, and it's not Thursday. I know that. I can smell Thursday all the way back to Wednesday when people put their garbage out. So . . . so . . . it must be Sunday! Sure! We got to walk in the park if it's Sunday!" She brightened up just as Sid Hogenson came in, red-faced and winded.

"Where was she?"

Faye smiled radiantly. "Hey, Sid, you and Muriel come for a walk with us?"

"She okay?"

Frank nodded wearily, sipping his coffee.

"You got to do something, Frank. You got to put a lock on that door."

"No."

"You got to. One day she's gonna wander out into that street and . . ."

"I won't do it, Sid! She's not an animal to be caged up, understand? She's not a child. She's a free person. She's Faye. I love her. Period."

"We're going to the park, aren't we, Sid? You and Muriel and Donald, and Frank and me and Bobby."

"Sure, Faye."

"Can we have ice cream, Frank?"

"Sure, honey."

"Donald and Bobby can play catch. Maybe later . . ."

Muriel Hogenson returned then. She closed her eyes in a relieved and weary smile when she saw Faye. "Okay, honey. Let's go upstairs and get dressed. Okay?"

Faye nodded happily, her hat bobbing. "Will you help me pick out clothes, Muriel?"

"Sure."

"We're going to the park."

"That's nice."

Leaning heavily on their table, the men watched the two

women cross the empty dance floor, go past the cold grill and the empty booths, each with its jaunty hat rack, and past the yellowing photographs of the cafe in its heyday, of patrons long gone waving and mugging for Marty Schwartz's camera.

When Faye's voice had faded down the hall and upstairs, Frank shook his head grimly. "I'm not leaving, Sid. No way. This is our neighborhood. We're staying. Together."

Sid spread his arms. "Neighborhood! What neighborhood? Take a look out there. Do you see any neighborhood anymore?"

Frank did not look outside. He looked at his friend. "The people will come back. The neighborhood will come back. It's cycles, Sid. You'll see. We just got to hang in a little longer."

"It won't happen. Uh-unh. And if you think you can make it happen just by staying here and holding out against Lacey and his goons . . ."

"And his money."

"Yeah, his money too, okay, but if you expect to make some miracle happen just by doing that, then you're as . . ." Sid stopped suddenly. He pressed his lips together and looked hard at the table.

"Go ahead. Say it. 'As crazy as she is,' right?"

"I didn't mean that, Frank."

Frank waved it away. "Well, maybe, maybe not. The law's on our side, don't forget."

"The *law!* Gimme a break!"

"Well, Lacey can't *make* us move. Not legally."

"Frank, Frank," Sid said quietly, "what Lacey decides to do about this place will have nothing to do with the law. You know that."

Frank turned to the window. He saw its new crack, saw

its thick dust, saw the chips and stains in its gilded letters: RILEYS' CAFE. He looked through it at the prowling bull-dozers, at the heaps of rubble, at the backhoes and power shovels clawing up the asphalt in jagged chunks. He looked at the glossy new sign with its picture of sleek and soaring towers: LACEY PLAZA.

Frank Riley looked at all of this, and he sighed. "Well," he said quietly, "he'd better get on with it, because Faye and me, we're stayin' right here."

Upstairs, Muriel Hogenson struggled to get Faye dressed. It was hard work. As soon as she got back to her apartment, Faye went straight to the shelf where she kept her albums and scrapbooks and picked one at random. It was packed with photographs of Bobby when he was no longer a child but not quite a man, and instantly Faye was swept back to mothering a person that age, with all the worries, all the joys.

"See?" she asked, as Muriel lifted first one arm and then the other to fit her sweater on. "Here he is with Ellen. She's two years *older* than he is, Muriel. Two years! Now, two years when you're thirty is one thing, but two years when you're . . ."

"See?" she asked, holding the album down so Muriel could look at it while she tied Faye's shoes. "Here he is last summer, when we took that trip to Myrtle Beach. See how big he is Muriel? Almost a man, now."

Muriel sighed and straightened up slowly. Her back hurt. "Was, dear," she said.

"Pardon?"

"Was. That's how big Bobby *was* when the picture was taken."

"Was . . ." Faye's world spun like one of those topsy-turvy rides at Coney Island. "But he's *just* like that! *Just* like that *now!*"

Muriel sighed again and turned to hang Faye's bathrobe in the closet. Bulldozers rumbled and growled in the distance. Something heavy crashed to earth, like thunder in the Montana hills Muriel remembered from childhood. The wire hangers in the closet shook and rattled.

She turned back to discover Faye looking at her oddly, frowning. "Muriel, do you mean to tell me that you don't *know* Bobby? Wouldn't recognize him if you passed him on the street?"

"Faye, I'm sorry. I'm just a little tired."

"Oh, Muriel, Muriel, you are *really* starting to slip! Poor thing!" She leaned forward and kissed the other woman tenderly on the cheek. "You should see a doctor, Muriel. There are things they can do, you know."

Muriel stood up. She felt more secure on her feet, on the square heels of her sensible shoes. She felt more . . . in control of things. "Faye, you come downstairs now. We'll have something to eat. Frank will cook you something nice."

"Not yet. Not quite yet."

"Soon, then."

"Soon."

"You won't . . . run away again?"

"You mean to do the marketing? Oh, no, Muriel dear. That's done. Don't you remember? No, I'll be down soon. In a few minutes."

Muriel shut the door softly and walked to the little window at the end of the hall. She leaned heavily, gratefully, on the sill. Her back hurt. Her feet hurt. She lit a cigarette.

Indifferent, she watched a long black limousine pass

slowly in the street below. She looked away, across East Ninth Street, across the ruins to a huge new sign: LACEY PLAZA.

She smoked.

2 —————————————————————

THE LIMOUSINE PASSED slowly along East Ninth Street and turned right on Avenue D. It drew into the curb about half-way down the block and stopped. It waited.

It was very long, very shiny, all silver and black. Even its windows were black, so dark that from outside only the chauffeur's hands could be seen on the steering wheel, gleaming like white fish, before they vanished into the depths of the car. Twin exhausts murmured. Behind the front bumper, a little pool of water formed on the steaming asphalt, the residue of the air conditioner that kept the interior as cool as an October afternoon.

From across the street, Carlos Chavez watched the arrival of the car with narrowed eyes. He smiled, nodding. He wiped a hand over his face, stripping off the sweat that had gathered on his brow and thin moustache. "See that car?" he said to his three companions. "Someday you gonna see *this* man in a car like that!"

17

The others responded with derision, as he knew they would. Al did his ape imitation, dragging his knuckles as he galloped in little circles. Ramirez tapped out some dance steps, tape machine shrieking on his shoulder. Poncho loosed manic howls of laughter. "What d'they do, Carlos? Give them cars away for scaring old ladies in pink hats? How many little old ladies you gotta scare, Carlos?"

"You wait," Carlos said, crossing the street and pointing back at them. "You wait and see!"

He straightened his shirt as he approached the limousine. He patted his face with a soiled handkerchief. He stood on the sidewalk beside the rear door until the window hummed open, then he leaned forward, hands on his knees. "Morning, Mr. Kovacs."

"Carlos." A large man in a pinstripe suit sat alone in the back seat. The corners of his mouth turned up in what may have been a smile. One eyelid twitched slightly. "I have a message for you from Mr. Lacey. In fact, I have two messages."

"Yes, sir. Always happy to hear from Mr. Lacey."

"First, he asked me to tell you how pleased he is with your work. In fact, if you and your, uh, associates are available, he would like your help elsewhere in the city. On another project."

"Oh, yes," Carlos smiled broadly, smoothing his sleek black hair. "We're available, Mr. Kovacs. Yes, sir. You just let me know where and when."

"Second"—Kovacs clicked open a thin attaché case on the velveteen seat— "I have another envelope for you."

Carlos reached for it, but Kovacs held the plain envelope just inside the window, inside the shadows of the car, and instead of extending his hand into the car, Carlos leaned on the roof.

Kovacs frowned. "Please don't touch the car."

"Sorry, sir."

"You're sweaty. Quite sweaty."

"Yes, sir." Carlos rubbed the roof with his sleeve.

"Here it is. It's a generous sum, as you'll see. It includes a bonus in advance."

Carlos smiled, leaning close. "Eight-seventeen East Ninth, correct?"

Kovacs said nothing. His nod was so slight it was almost no movement at all.

"Consider it done, Mr. Kovacs."

"Speed, Carlos. That is what the bonus is for. Time is of the essence."

"Right you are, sir. Thank you. And tell Mr. Lacey thank you, too!" Carlos raised the envelope, but the window was already purring up; Kovacs had already said "Office" to the driver; the car was already pulling away.

Carlos swaggered back across the street.

"We ready?" Al stood with his hands on his hips, watching him come.

"Yeah," Carlos said. He spat a thin stream into the gutter.

"So what is it? What's goin' down here?"

Carlos patted his breast pocket. "Little packages for the good folks in 817 East Ninth."

"You a delivery boy then, Carlos? That what you are?"

Carlos's eyes narrowed. He pointed at Al, who pursed his lips in mock surprise, jogging from one foot to the other. "I might deliver you somethin' you won't like, Al, my man." He patted Al's cheek. "On the other hand, I might deliver you somethin' you *will* like, if those folks move out real quick."

"Ah," Poncho smiled, opening his hands to catch imaginary blessings from heaven. "Mr. Kovacs! A little message from the main man."

"Right you are." Carlos smiled at each of them. His mouth smiled, but his eyes did not smile. He felt nothing for any of them, but he was wary. He knew what his Crusaders were capable of. He had seen too many people too badly hurt not to be wary of the Crusaders.

He smiled and nodded, caressing the aluminum baseball bat that he had left leaning against the wall.

Carlos Chavez lived by his wits, by his cunning. Except for his tropical fish, which he sometimes watched by the hour, he lived alone. Usually he moved alone. He brought the Crusaders together only when there were certain jobs to be done. They met; they did what was necessary; they separated. That was the way they wanted it, especially Carlos.

He could not remember when he had felt anything, really *felt* anything for anybody. He disdained people who had allowed themselves to be softened by feelings. What *was* affection, after all? Just another way of controlling you.

"We go, Carlos? Or you gonna stand in a trance all day?"

"We go. *We go!*" He flung out his arms and they scattered, barking like jackals, into the labyrinth of rubble, headed for 817 East Ninth, and Rileys' Cafe.

Halfway there, at the corner of a tenement being consumed by cranes, Ramirez halted, pointed across the street, and began to slap his belly, hopping in gleeful circles. The others shoved forward, squinting into the sunlight and the dust.

On the other side of the street, a young woman was going home. She walked slowly and awkwardly, carrying a little bag of groceries that she had bought in the supermarket four blocks away. She leaned back to offset the weight in her swelling womb. Her long black hair fell straight, almost to her waist. She looked hot, and pale, and tired, and undernourished.

Carlos touched Ramirez and Al on the arms and gestured to the woman, and then he beckoned to Poncho to go ahead with him to 817.

Radio turned high, swaying, prancing, Ramirez and Al crossed the street and fell into step behind the young woman. She ignored them. Her eyes narrowed, her mouth hardened, but her pace did not change.

Ramirez mimicked her walk. He leaned back. He stuck his belly out. "Hey, Marisa!" he shouted over the clamor of the tape and the bulldozers. "Look here! I'm pregnant too! Whatdya know, a miracle!"

The young woman looked straight ahead, walking slowly and steadily. The entrance to her apartment building was only a hundred yards away, now. Ninety-five. Ninety...

"Hey! Hey, Senorita Esquivel," Al shouted, turning in little tapping circles with his arms raised like a Spanish dancer, "you finish that baby, you wanna make another, eh? Olé!"

Eighty yards... Seventy-five... But the laughter was coming from in front as well as behind, and she saw that there were two others waiting for her with open arms on the steps of the apartment, holding the door wide.

So they had a key to the front door. They probably had keys to the apartments, too.

She knew who they were and why they had come.

Carlos was grinning broadly. "Welcome, Chiquita! We been waiting for you, you see? Allow me to hold the door open for you. Such a pretty and very wealthy lady should not have to exert herself. That is why we have come, Senorita Esquivel, to help you."

Lounging against the railing, Poncho tried to pat her

belly as she passed, but she slapped his hand away and went inside, stepping hard on the toe of Carlos's sneaker. They all followed her, laughing, kicking up the old, loose ceramic tiles. Ramirez's radio boomed in the vestibule. She hesitated, then checked her mailbox.

"Empty?" Carlos asked. "Aw, too bad, chiquita. He ain't comin' back, you see? Take it from me, Carlos. I know. And that is why you should be *so* happy to see me, because I have for you"—he drew a long envelope from his jacket—"the means of in-de-pendence! Believe me, Senorita Marisa, *this* is the letter you been waiting for!"

Her name was typed on it: *Marisa Esquivel, 3C.*

She swept past him to the stairs. They were long flights, because of the high ceilings in the old building. She went slowly, one hand holding her belly, the other cradling the bag of groceries. Echoing inside the stairwell the raucous laughter and the clamor of the radio made her head ache. When she reached the third floor, she was gasping for breath and she had to stand still a minute until her head cleared.

They crowded around her at the door of her apartment, and Carlos held the envelope close in front of her eyes so that she couldn't see to get the key into the lock. At last, when she opened the door and tried to shut it from the inside, he kicked it so hard that it slammed back against the little table and her plaster statue of St. Anthony. Statue and table smashed to the floor.

She whirled and clouted Carlos across the ear with her purse, hard. "Get out of here!"

He kept smiling his cold smile. He took one small and menacing step towards her, his shoe crunching in the fragments of the plaster saint. He threw the envelope of money on the couch. "You just accepted Mr. Lacey's money. I saw you do it, right? Now you can afford to buy a new saint and move to Brooklyn. Start packing, Chiquita. *Start packing!"* He went out and slammed the door.

Marisa rushed over and bolted it, and then, falling to her knees in the midst of the fragments of the little statue that Hector had given her for good luck before he left, she burst into tears.

"One down," Carlos said to his gang in the hall. "Now we go for two. Mister..." He consulted a crumpled list. "Mister Mason Baylor. Four C."

Up the stairs they went, shouting, kicking the walls of empty apartments, the radio blaring. When they reached 4C, Carlos made exaggerated gestures for silence, and Ramirez turned the machine down until it was barely a whisper, softer even than the hiss of the fluorescent orange paint can that Poncho was using to decorate the walls.

Carlos tapped. "Hello there, Mister Baylor."

No answer.

"Hell-o-o-o. Do I have the residence of Mr. Mason Baylor, famous artist?"

No reply.

Carlos dug the master key out of his hip pocket and opened the door, only to discover that it was chained inside. "He *is* there! Just shy, I guess. Here ya go, Rembrandt! Buy enough paints to last forever." He flipped the envelope through the crack, only to have the door slammed shut and the envelope come skidding back out underneath.

"Hey! Hey, amigo. That ain't polite. You *hear* me?"

He kicked once, twice. The bottom panel of the door splintered open, and through the hole they heard a scream and glimpsed a woman's ankle.

Poncho dropped to his knees and lunged, groping for the ankle with his arm through the door up to his shoulder. He uttered exaggerated animal sounds—growls and snarls and snorts—and then a yelp of pain as something crashed down on his hand. He yanked it out, cursing.

The others laughed. "Hey!" Carlos called. "You in there! Tell your boyfriend to take the money and leave. Got that? Simple enough?" He kicked the door again, cracking a second panel.

"Two down," he said to the others as they went back towards the stairs. "Three to go. Hey, Poncho, what'd she hit you with?"

"A log! A two-by-four!"

"It's whatcha get for messin' around. How many times I gotta tell ya, Poncho?" Carlos patted the big man's cheek. "Don't grab for the ladies, remember? Ask *permission* first."

They headed downstairs, Poncho spraying obscene suggestions on the walls all the way.

Behind, in the apartment with the broken door, Pamela Gruber shuddered; she could still feel that hand on her ankle. She didn't need that. She didn't need bulldozers rumbling all day outside her window, spewing fumes. She didn't need whistles and catcalls from the construction workers every time she went out to shop. She didn't need any more of Mason Baylor's dumb paintings. Come to think of it, she didn't really need Mason anymore either, with all his moods, all his artist's arrogance.

Besides, she had taken a look inside the envelope Carlos had thrown on the couch. There was money inside.

A lot of money.

The gang headed downstairs, to the basement.

There was only one tiny apartment here, next to the furnace room. A yellowing piece of paper in a brass clip on the door said HARRY NOBLE, ALMOST WORLD CHAMPION.

Carlos tapped. "We're gonna have some fun here." He

tapped again, louder this time. "Hey, champ, you in there? Open up. It's your manager. I wanna make you rich."

Carlos put his ear close to the door, but there was no answer. He shrugged and used his master key. The door swung open.

"What's *this?*" Ramirez said. "What the hell is this, *toy*land?"

The only light in the dingy room filtered through filthy windows at street level, and from an old TV, blaring an advertisement. A mighty toy truck growled its way across the screen. Scattered around the floor, lying on the table and on a rickety workbench, were dozens of other toys, all battery-driven trucks and tanks, jets and helicopters, boats and sailing ships on tiny wheels, and many unearthly toys as well—space ships, space stations, flying saucers. Most were assembled, but some were not. Several waited in cellophane-wrapped boxes.

"Hey! Champ!" Carlos advanced, kicking toys out of the way. Around the walls were shelves of boxing trophies, dozens of them, and when he got no answer, Carlos reached up with his baseball bat and swept a row of these to the floor.

Al laughed. He grabbed one and hurled it through the TV screen. The set sputtered, sparked, went silent. "Ya got less to move now, champ! Might as well come out and get started."

Off the main room was a tiny kitchen on one side and a tiny bedroom on the other—no place to hide at all, except in the bedroom closet. Grinning, Carlos pointed to the closet door, and then to a basket of ceramic tiles on the table in the living room. Poncho grabbed this basket and hurled it against the closet door, smashing the tiles into a thousand pieces. "Just a warning, champ," Carlos said, laying the envelope on the bureau. "Remember, you ain't no world champion and you never was. Take the money and *run*. Vamos!"

"Three down," he said, as the gang headed back upstairs. "Now the *real* fun begins."

For a long time after the Crusaders had gone, there was silence in the basement apartment. Then the closet door clicked open a tiny crack, widened, swung back. Harry Noble emerged. He was a huge man, and although his shoulders were more stooped and less muscular than they had been, they were powerful still. He carried his hands awkwardly in front of him, and he looked frightened and confused, as if he wanted someone to tell him what to do.

Balloon tires on a moon-module toy purred at his feet. Harry picked up the little machine and cradled it in his huge palm. He tried to turn it off, but the switch was broken, and so he opened a door in its belly and removed its batteries. "Repairs required," he said, carrying it over to the shaky workbench under the window. And then, his scarred brows wrinkling with the effort of concentration, he began to check the other toys as well and to replace the trophies on their shelves, carefully, one by one.

In the process he discovered the packet of money Carlos had left on the bureau. He looked at it and tossed it unopened into the garbage can in the kitchen.

Meanwhile, the Crusaders had reached the main floor and burst into the kitchen of Rileys' Cafe, where they found Frank toasting raisin bread and frying eggs on his hot plate.

"Hey!" Frank shouted.

They shouldered past him.

"Once over lightly, pops," Carlos said.

"Sunny-side up," Ramirez grinned. "And coffee with *lots* of sugar. *Sweet!*" He swept a line of glasses off a shelf, sending them smashing to the floor. Poncho tried to spray something across the refrigerator, but he had run out of paint and so he tossed the empty spray can into Frank's fried eggs.

"You punks get outta here!" Frank shouted.

Carlos pushed him, once, twice, hard, and Frank staggered backward through the swinging door and out into the cafe, still shouting. The Crusaders crowded through behind him.

Muriel and Faye were sitting with Sid at their usual table. Radiant, Faye rose with her arms spread. "Bobby! Donald! How nice! You and your friends want some lunch? Sit down, boys. Take this table."

Muriel tugged her arm. "Faye, that isn't Bobby. And that isn't my Donald, either."

But Faye was pulling away from her, going towards Carlos with her arms outstretched. "Give your mother a kiss!"

Ramirez spun in little circles, convulsed in laughter, slapping his knees. Al grinned. Poncho, wriggling close, said, "Yeah, yeah. And give your daddy a kiss, too. Mmmmmm."

Carlos took Faye by the elbows and propelled her back into her chair. "I ain't Bobby, lady! I *am* your lucky day. Here . . . you . . . go!" And out of his pocket he drew the last two envelopes, one addressed to Mr. and Mrs. Sid Hogenson, and the other to Mr. and Mrs. Frank Riley.

"Don't open that!" Frank shouted, but Faye had already torn the end off the envelope, shaken several $100 bills into a little pile on the table, and began to toss them like a Caesar salad.

"Hallelujah!"

"Faye, don't touch it! Don't touch it!"

"She *took* it, man!" Carlos patted Frank on the cheek,

and then turned to the others. "You saw her take it, didn't you?"

"Sure, man," Ramirez said.

"She *took* it," Al said.

"So," Carlos turned back to Frank, "what that means is that you are outta here by tomorrow morning, poppa."

"You think so?"

"Yeah."

"You *think* so?"

"Yeah!"

"I'll show you who's outta here! I'm callin' the cops!" Frank lurched towards the phone, but he was cut off by a wall of bodies—Ramirez, Al, and Poncho. "Okay," he said, holding up his hands, very pale. "I don't call the cops. *Get Faye outta here!"* he whispered to the Hogensons. *"Please!"*

Muriel took the old woman by the shoulders, half lifting her from her chair. "Time for your medicine, Faye, honey. Come on, now."

"Bobby. . ."

"Bobby's all right. He's fine. He and Frank are just going to have a little talk for a while. That right. . . Bobby?"

"Sure," Carlos said. "That's right. You run along now, mamacita."

Very pale, the Hogensons hurried her out of the cafe, one on each side.

"Listen, now. . ." Carlos began when she had gone, spreading his arms.

"No, *you* listen!" Frank was trembling, but his gaze was level. "I talk, you listen. One, you stay away from my wife. Two, you stay out of our building. Three, you tell Lacey his money stinks! You tell him he will never, never send enough money, or enough punks like you, to make us move. He can't scare me, and neither can you. You tell him that!"

Carlos's eyes were flat. The eyes of a dead fish. He took one menacing step towards Frank, as he had earlier towards Marisa, and then stopped himself. His grin broadened slowly. His arms spread slowly, palms out. "Aww. You kill my head, man. You mean money's not a good reason to move? Huh? That what you mean, poppa? We give you a good reason then."

Catlike, he twisted and swept his bat into the glass shelves of dishes above the counter. They crashed and toppled, cascading over the stools and onto the floor. "That good enough reason for you? No?" He pointed at Al, who seized a broken chair leg and began methodically to smash the light fixtures, laughing crazily as the shards of fluorescent glass rained down on him. *"That* enough reason for you, poppa? No?" Carlos pointed to Poncho, who took a little stroll around the cafe looking for a suitable target, his arms outstretched as if he were dancing an innocent Spanish dance, coming to a halt at last before one of the photographs, a picture of Rileys' Cafe as it had been in '46, when Faye and Frank had taken it over from Faye's father. There it was, with the new neon sign proud in the front, RILEYS' CAFE, and underneath, Faye and Frank when they were young and full of hope, and surrounded by old friends and customers, smiling men in their floppy trousers and broad hats, women in flowered dresses with their hair in buns.

"No. Please," Frank said.

But Poncho had already gently lifted the picture off its hook. Grinning at Frank, he brought it crashing down on the corner of one of the tables. Pane and frame shattered. The photograph ripped across the middle. Poncho hurled it against the wall, still grinning.

Frank swore and lunged at him, but Carlos pinned the old man easily, dragging him through the front entrance and locking the door in his face.

"Go!" he said to the Crusaders, and they launched into an orgy of destruction, smashing everything that could be pounded to bits with table legs, or mangled against a wall, or simply kicked apart.

Horrified and helpless, Frank stared at this mayhem through the front window, until a chair hurtled out, showering him with glass. He reeled back into the street, an absurd and pathetic figure in his apron and cook's hat, shouting, "Help us! Somebody please help us!", right into the path of a very long black limousine with smoked windows.

Fortunately, the car was going slowly. Frank bumped harmlessly against the fender and fell across the hood. "Help . . ." He squinted at the glinting windshield, trying to see into the back seat; then he pounded the hood so hard he dented it. "You! Lacey! You proud of this, Lacey? Come on out and face me like a man!" He groped down the side of the car and beat on the rear window with both fists. "You won't buy me out! You hear that, Lacey? And you can't scare me, either! You can tear it all down, but we'll still be here! We're a hell of a lot tougher than you are, Lacey! You hear that! You hear . . ."

The smoked window purred down to reveal a smiling, well-dressed, overweight man with a nervous twitch in his right eye. "Mr. Riley, do you really think Mr. Lacey would come down here?" Kovacs smiled and shook his head. He spoke into the intercom, and the car slid forward, smooth as a great ship. "Take the money," he said as the window rose again. "Later on, Mr. Riley, when time has run out, there won't be any money at all."

The car passed Rileys' Cafe just as a second chair sailed

through the other plate-glass window, showering street and car with glass. It accelerated abruptly and sped away.

The Crusaders came through the windowless front of the cafe laughing, slapping one another on the back. Al reached up with his knife and slit the awning into ribbons as he passed. When he saw Frank standing stunned in the middle of the street, Poncho started towards him, but Carlos pulled him back. "Enough," he said. He shouted to Frank, "Take the money, poppa! We have to come back here again, somebody might get hurt, you understand? *Take the money!*"

Frank felt very heavy, and tired, and *old,* older than he had ever felt. He realized that he was stooped over, that his arms were hanging like rags. He looked at Carlos. He straightened his back and shook his head. "No damn way," he said.

Mike O'Malley was one of the cops who came.

He was an old friend of the Rileys. For many, many years East Ninth Street had been his beat, and he had chatted with Frank and Faye every day over a Coke or a coffee, his cap on the table and his big shoes comfortably hoisted onto a second chair.

He was a lieutenant now, and his duties kept him close to the precinct office, but occasionally when calls came involving his old neighborhood and old friends, he climbed into a squad car. He arrived now at Rileys' Cafe with a sergeant half his age who came in through the front window saying, "Shoo-ee! Did they trash *this* place!"

They stood with Frank in the middle of the shambles, listening to his story with their caps on the backs of their heads. Occasional squawks came from their car.

"So?" Frank said. "So? You guys know who did it. Carlos did it! Carlos and Ramirez and . . ."

"Yeah. We know, Frank," Mike O'Malley said.

"So go get 'em!"

"You really *want* us to do that?"

"Of *course* I want ya to do that. What d'ya think . . ."

"Got witnesses?"

"Sure. The Hogensons were sitting right there. Faye was . . ." He stopped.

Mike O'Malley looked down. "Faye," he said.

"Okay," Frank said. *"I'll* testify."

"Sure. You testify. Then what?"

"Then you put 'em away!"

"Wrong. Then they have six witnesses all testifying they were someplace else. And when they get off, you know what happens. They come back and hit you again. Harder."

"Well, you guys *protect* me!"

"Frank, we can't be here all the time. They *can.*"

Frank looked from one tired, grim face to the other. He knew they were right. Next time it would be worse. Next time they might hurt Faye.

Mike put an arm around his shoulders. "Listen, Frank. I'm your friend, right?"

Frank nodded.

"Let me give you some advice. Off the record, okay? Leave. Just leave. Take Faye and go someplace where these punks can't bother you anymore."

"No."

"Life's too short, Frank."

The old man looked up from the chair into which he had slumped. He was pale. He was gasping a little. One fist was pressed into the center of his chest. But his eyes were steely slits. "Yeah," he said. "Life *is* too short, Mike. It's too short not to fight for what you know is right. See that money over there? Scattered around? Take it with you. It's evidence. Besides, it clutters the place up. Makes it smell bad."

For a long time after the two policemen had gone, Frank sat alone in the ruin of his cafe. He looked at the bulldozers and trucks grumbling about their business of destruction in the lots across the street, but he did not really see them. He heard water trickling from a shattered tap, and someone calling, and the rattle of pneumatic hammers in the construction sites, but he did not really hear them. What he was seeing were the faces of old comrades who had stuck to their guns, who had died young so that others might grow old with respect and dignity. What he was listening to was the echo of ghostly detonations, and the crackle of rapid fire, and those men joining him one by one, saying, *"No damn way!"*

He picked up a broken table leg. He shifted his chair so that he faced the shattered door.

Mason Baylor came back to 817 East Ninth at dusk.

He had lived there four months, attracted to the neighborhood by falling rents, and to that building by its big, well-lighted rooms, ideal for studios. At first, preoccupied by his painting, he had been as indifferent to the rest of the building as he was to other tenants, but gradually he began to notice details—each newel post, each cornice, each embellishment on the elaborate facade. Slowly he came to appreciate the grace of the spiral fire escape, the elegance of the stilted arches above the windows. He began to make paintings of the old place, and the more he painted it the more he liked it. "Sure, it's old," he would say when Pamela complained about living there. "But it's also beautiful, this place. It *is*. It's worth, well, it's worth *saving*."

He had surprised himself. He had never thought of saving anything before, but the more he looked at his paintings, the more the idea obsessed him. For four months he had painted that neighborhood, painted the reality before his eyes—the shambling old hulks that had once been gracious buildings, the mounds of rubble that had once been homes. He had all his paintings, four months' worth, because no one bought them. "Dark and gloomy," people said when he tried to sell them on the street. "Depressing."

Gallery owners declined to show them. So there they still were, lining the walls of his studio, the only record left of that once bright and bustling neighborhood. All the buildings in his pictures were long since gone, leveled by cranes, bulldozed for Lacey Plaza.

Only 817 East Ninth remained.

As the wreckers drew closer, Mason Baylor got more desperate, more frantic. Protecting the place obsessed him. He did several foolish things. He opened his window and taunted the wrecking crew. No one paid any attention. The trucks rumbled on. He crept over at night and let the air out of big tires on the site, until he got caught, and was fined, and sternly warned by the judge. He tried to stop Gus's bulldozer, *Chief Broom,* by sitting down in front of it, but the big man had climbed calmly down and lifted Mason out of harm's way, like a small child. He had even tried to get in to see Martin Lacey himself and had ended up sitting for two days in the office lobby of Lacey Inc., ignored. "Crank," he heard one of Lacey's planners say as he passed with a roll of blueprints under his arm. His companion had glanced over at Mason's long black hair and beard, at his paint-splattered jeans, and replied, "Preservationist."

That remark took him next morning to the Commission of Historical Landmarks. He had waited most of the day there as well, but late in the afternoon he was taken in to see Alma Thompson, the chairperson. She was a formidable, gray-haired lady with glasses dangling on a gold chain around her neck. She wore a stern suit and had a hard and direct gaze, but she was honest looking, and Mason liked her. In a half hour of impassioned pleading, he had persuaded her to drive with him to 817 East Ninth Street and examine this historic building, an ideal candidate for preservation. The board *did* have the power to preserve unique specimens, didn't it?

Ms. Thompson assured him that it did.

And so, late in the afternoon, they drove down Avenue D in her gray Jaguar. "You see?" Mason flung his arm out toward the fields of rubble, and the dusty battered machines, and the tired workers straggling back to their pickup trucks beside the trailers. "Official vandalism. We have no respect for the past, do you know that, Ms. Thompson?"

The lady maneuvering the Jaguar in her gloved hands smiled skeptically. "Well, some old buildings, Mr. Baylor, really are without much merit. And, when they reach a certain stage of deterioration . . ."

"Not this one! No, ma'am! Oh, it may need a little paint here and there, a little refurbishing, but this building is *sound*. Well cared for. You'll see."

They rounded the corner onto East Ninth Street, and 817 loomed ahead, lonely and mournful amidst the ruins and the long shadows of afternoon.

Ms. Thompson squinted doubtfully through her glasses. "It certainly doesn't look . . ."

"Just the light! When you get close, you'll see the details. You'll see the *potential*."

But when the Jaguar slid to a halt beside the entrance, Mason's heart sank. The door hung on one hinge. Glass from its shattered panels spilled down the concrete steps and onto the sidewalk. Tiles from the mosaic floor in the vestibule had been kicked out into the gutter; the Jaguar's tires crunched them as it drew up to the curb. The lights at the entrance had been smashed and knocked crooked, and crude graffiti had been spray-painted across the bricks in fluorescent orange.

Heartsick, Mason got out and stared.

Ms. Thompson picked her way through broken glass to examine what had been the front of the cafe. She hurried back. "Is this some kind of *joke,* Mr. Baylor?"

"This has all just happened! I swear..."

"There's a *man,*" Ms. Thompson said quietly, eyes shifting nervously. "A man sitting in the dark in that *place*. And he's holding a large stick!"

"Ms. Thompson..."

"What you have here is a slum. A ruin. How could you *possibly* think I could recommend this building?" She started back around the long nose of the Jaguar.

"Ms. Thompson, please, wait a minute. Look at those mouldings, that cornice, the lines of the roof! Step back a bit, Ms. Thompson, so you can appreciate the proportions. Why, there's *style* there, don't you think?"

"Perhaps once."

"Dignity?"

"Please!"

"Well," Mason shrugged. "It was in much better shape this morning. Really. Maybe if I just drew you a few sketches..." He whipped out a felt pen and headed for a blank space of wall.

"No!" she called firmly, shaking her head. "No, I don't think so, Mr. Baylor. We do have a minimum standard. The building must be fundamentally sound, intact, and livable."

"But it *is* livable. People live here. *I* live here."

"Mr. Baylor, I'd like to be able to help, but this building has gone far past anything the commission might do to restore it. It's hopeless, I'm sorry to say. And as for the neighborhood, well, it really doesn't exist anymore, does it."

A pickup truck rattled past, swirling a thick cloud of dust over and through Ms. Thompson's Jaguar.

When she had gone, Mason Baylor shrugged and shook his head grimly. He walked along the front of 817 East Ninth, staring at the wreckage, sweeping broken glass and tiles into the gutter with the side of his foot. When he came to the yawning front of the cafe, he was startled by a hoarse voice from the shadows.

"Forget something? Forget to break a cup, maybe? That why you're back? Well, come and try. I'm ready for ya this time!"

Peering in, Mason saw Frank Riley rising slowly from the only unbroken chair in the place. He was gripping a table leg in both hands and swinging it in little circles, like a batter stepping up to the plate.

"Hey! Wait a minute! I live here!"

Frank moved towards him, squinting. "Who the hell are you?"

"Mason Baylor. I live in 4C."

"Oh yeah." The end of the table leg dropped. "You're the squatter in the Moscowitzes' old place."

"What d'ya mean *squatter?* I live here! I pay rent. I've just been trying to *save* this place." Mason stepped in through the front window.

Frank grunted and sat back down. "Yeah? Well, you're a little late."

"Why'd they *do* this?"

The old man laughed bitterly. "Where you been, kid? They want us outta here, doncha know that? Doncha know about *development?*"

"But why pick on you?"

"Not just me. Go take a look at your own place. Probably looks just like this."

"They were *up* there?"

"Yeah, they were up there. They were everywhere."

"Why didn't you stop them?"

"Are you kidding? Look at me. Twice your age. Three times, maybe. Anyway, I tried. Goddammit, I tried! Maybe if I'd had a little help . . ."

"Is Pamela all right? They didn't hurt her . . ." Mason was backing towards the door into the hall, tripping over wreckage.

The old man shrugged. "Who's Pamela?"

Mason ran for the stairs.

3 ──────────────────────────────

FRANK RILEY SAT motionless in the growing darkness, listening to the laughter of Carlos and the others from the ruins across the street. His resolve ebbed with the fading light. He felt old. For the first time he knew being old did not mean to be tired; it meant not to have faith. And for the first time, alone in his ruined cafe, Frank Riley did not have faith.

He still had courage. He just did not have faith.

Funny, he thought. Faith was something you didn't think much about until after it was gone—like having both arms and legs and then losing one. He had always had faith, he guessed—faith that no matter how bad things got, they would work out somehow.

But now, suddenly, he didn't feel that anymore. The future was as gray and bleak and sterile as the ruin that Lacey had made of the old neighborhood, and in the face

of it now, in the darkness, faith to confront it had drained
away.

So, when Sid and Muriel came down from upstairs,
Frank guessed what was coming. He saw it in the guilty
way Sid looked around and nudged a fragment of teacup
with his toe, and said, "Animals! They sure had fun, didn't
they?" He saw it in their embarrassment, in the way that
both of them avoided his eyes.

"You took the money. You took Lacey's money."
Frank's voice was like a hurt child's.

Sid pressed his lips together and folded his arms. He
looked at the floor. "We called Donald," he said. "He made
the arrangements. There's a truck on its way."

"Right now?"

"Yeah, Frank. We're going to Hoboken. There's a
retirement home. Here. Look." Sid produced a brochure
and offered it to Frank, but the older man ignored it.

"It's time you went too, Frank," Muriel said. "For
Faye's sake. She deserves something better. With that
money, you could buy it for her."

Frank shook his head. "She'd die anyplace else! That
what you want? You want to kill her?"

"Don't talk crazy. We're your friends. You know that."

"No. I don't know that. I used to know it, but I don't
now."

Suddenly a cheer went up from across the street, and
Carlos and the Crusaders appeared on the sidewalk, laughing, swatting hands, ushering a large moving van into the
curb. They applauded as two muscular men in caps descended from the cab and opened the rear door. They applauded as they began to haul out dollies and quilted pads.
They cheered and applauded as Donald arrived and
propped open the door of 817 for the movers.

Frank lifted his chin. "Hear that? Just what they want."

"Yeah, well it's what we want too, Frank. Honest, we gotta go now."

Muriel laid a hand on Frank's shoulder. "Come upstairs, Frank. Please. I'll show you about Faye's medicine. After tonight, you're gonna have to give it to her."

Heavily, Frank got up and followed her.

Behind him came the movers, like large bears under their pads. And behind the movers came Donald, who had once been Bobby's best friend . . .

Mason Baylor arrived at his apartment, 4C, to find the bottom door panel kicked out and a chair wedged under the knob inside.

"Pamela? *Pamela?* Open up! Let me in!"

The chair scuffed across the floor, and the chains rattled. The door swung back. Pamela stepped aside as he entered. She had been lugging a suitcase towards the door. Another packed suitcase sat waiting beside her, and a third lay open on the bed.

"Don't touch me, Mason."

"What?"

She shook her head, avoiding his gaze. "I've made up my mind. I'm leaving."

"Pam . . ."

"Do you want to help me or not?"

"Pam, this whole thing is stupid."

She whirled around. "Stupid? *Stupid?* If you'd been here when those thugs came you wouldn't think it was so stupid!"

"Did they hurt you?"

"No, they didn't *hurt* me. They were just the last straw, that's all." She started to sob then, jerking the zipper of the last suitcase shut. "I took the wine. It was my wine, anyway. And I took the Sun Ra tapes and the clock radio." She hauled the suitcase past the splintered door and into the hall.

"Look. I'll get a new door, okay? Thick. Oak. With bigger chains. And a peephole."

She pushed past him, returning for the other bags. "It's not the door, Mason. It's you! You and your fascination with this . . . this *place!*"

"I like it here."

"Exactly! It's dark and depressing."

"It's not! It's reality!"

She pulled the third bag into the hall. "These are the eighties. Nobody's interested in reality anymore."

"Oh no? Then what about *that?"*

"What?"

"That letter. From Corbeil Galleries."

"Mason, that's a *form* letter, for godsake! What a child you are! There'll be at least a hundred artists with that same letter tacked up in pathetic little studios, just like this one."

"It just takes a little time. You know that. Galleries are slow."

"Slow! You got that letter last October." She pointed at him. "Do yourself a favor. Admit it. It's time for you to quit."

"How would you know?"

"Because you told me yourself, that's how. You *said* you were going nowhere."

"I did? When?"

"Night before last. You were sneering at everything— Neo-geo, Analytical Deconstruction, Hard-edge. Trendy, you said they were. Shallow. Superficial. Here today, gone tomorrow. You said *you* wouldn't do that sort of stuff for any amount of money. So what do *you* do? You try to be the Andrew Wyeth of the East Village!"

"I was depressed. *You* get that way sometimes after a bad audition."

"No wonder I get depressed, living in this dump." Pamela pulled her bags along the corridor and started down the stairs. "Look, why don't you just go back to your father and sell RVs or vans or whatever they're called? And you know something else?"

"What?"

"I think you're kind of weird anyway."

"Why?"

"Because you never painted me *nude,* that's why."

"Pam, we can fix that." Mason leaned over the railing, shouting down the stairwell. "We can fix that right now!" But there was no response except for the rhythmic thudding of suitcases hitting the steps as she descended.

He ran back into the studio and opened the front window, leaning out just in time to see a taxi slow down and pull in to the curb behind the moving van as Pamela emerged from the front door. "Pam, don't do it!" he shouted. Perhaps the noise of the wreckers drowned him out. Perhaps she heard but pretended she didn't. He cupped his hands to his mouth. He wanted to shout, *I love you,* but somehow the words wouldn't come. Instead he shouted, "You'll be famous! Someday you'll be a famous model!" But it was too late. The cab driver had loaded her bags into the trunk while she climbed into the back seat. The doors slammed, and she was gone.

Gone with the wind. Gone with her Sun Ra tapes and her clock radio.

And gone with something else that Mason would never miss because he hadn't known about it: the packet of money Carlos had tossed into the studio. The packet with Mason's name on the envelope.

For the rest of the evening, Mason Baylor thought about

what she had said. He opened a beer and thought about it. He opened another beer and thought some more about it, staring at the canvases around the walls, and at the unfinished one waiting on his easel. The more he looked, the more he thought, the more depressed he got.

His work was derivative, clumsy, amateurish. Gloomy. All his paintings were failures, doomed to oblivion just like the neighborhood itself, just like the building in which he sat.

A great hollow place opened inside him, where his stomach should have been, and to fill it he had another beer. And then another.

By nightfall, he had begun to hate the paintings passionately. They crowded him like malicious living things. For an hour he beat them back, kicking them and flinging them into the corners of the apartment, but they kept creeping close, mocking him. At last, he lurched over and opened a window.

In the apartment directly below, Marisa Esquivel huddled inside a blanket. All afternoon, since being harassed by Carlos and the others, since being touched by the despicable Poncho, she had sat like that, trembling, staring at the envelope on the couch where Carlos had tossed it. She hadn't eaten lunch. Her few groceries lay where she had dropped them—in the middle of the floor.

At last, late in the evening, she rose, took the bag into her tiny kitchen, and poured herself a glass of milk. She padded barefoot into her bedroom and adjusted a picture on her bureau so that she could see it clearly—a picture of a handsome young man with a guitar, grinning broadly. Across a bottom corner was written: *My Marisa I Love you passionately no matter how far we are apart. Yours Hector.*

Sipping her milk, caressing the baby in her womb, Marisa gazed at this picture. He had promised to write to her every week, and he hadn't done it. He had promised to call her once a month, and she had never heard from him. He had promised to send money, and she had never received a cent.

And yet, she loved him still. He was so handsome, and so full of life! And his music was wonderful! When his band played the fast pieces, she could not stand still. She had to dance. And sometimes, when he played the slow pieces late at night, just for her, she wept. It wasn't easy being a musician, being the leader of the band. She knew that. She knew he had to go where his work took him. She knew that sometimes he would be away for weeks. And she knew also that one day he would come sailing in as if nothing had happened, as if he had not been away for half a year, but was just coming home from a practice. And she would be so happy to see him that in spite of everything, she would run to throw her arms around him.

Frightened and full of longing, Marisa clenched her fist and punched Hector's picture softly on the point of his handsome chin.

At that instant, something crashed on her windowsill. She screamed and covered her belly with both arms, whirling around.

A dark, crumpled painting of old buildings teetered for an instant on her outside sill and then toppled off into the night. Seconds later, another canvas landed on the same spot. Then another plummeted past, and then another, sailing over the street and the corner lot, then another, spinning in the opposite direction.

Horrified, Marisa saw these paintings drop into the darkness. She switched off her light and ran to the window, cupping her hands against the pane, straining to see exactly where every one of Mason Baylor's paintings fell to earth.

"Things come apart," Harry Noble said to himself. "Things come apart *all* the time. You gotta keep 'em together." He frowned, creasing the heavy scar tissue across his brow. "You gotta keep 'em together, because otherwise . . ."

From his basement rooms, Harry had brought glue, a small hammer, and a wastebasket full of all the broken tiles that he had gathered as the mosaic floors in the halls of the old building loosened with age and neglect. Now, crouched in the dimming light of the vestibule, he was striving patiently to reconstruct the floor of the main entrance from his various bits and pieces. It was impossible. Only someone desperate and obsessed would attempt such a job. Most tiles had cracked as dirt and debris had accumulated under them. Carlos and his Crusaders had kicked up the loose ones, shattering them down the steps and sidewalk. The original pattern was hopelessly scrambled, but Harry remembered that the number of the building, 817, had once been set in gleaming black tiles in the center of the vestibule, and it was this number that he was now laboring patiently to reconstruct.

The work was not going well. The light was poor, the floor was bumpy, the fragments did not fit together. Also, Harry kept forgetting. "Eight, one, seven," he repeated to himself, frowning with concentration. "Eight, one, seven."

But then, he would think about something else; he would think about growing up not far from there, strolling past that very building with his friends on their way to the gym on a Saturday afternoon. Or he would think about the many times he had climbed through the ropes and raised his gloved fists for the crowds, doing a little dance. Or he would think about Sally. Sally. . .

And then, first thing he knew, he would be kneeling there in the vestibule again, in the faint light. He would have to get up and go outside to look again at the front of the building. "Eight, one, seven . . ."

By the time he ran out of black tiles, he hadn't even completed the *8*. He had made only a dark, roundish mass of fragments, which, Harry saw as he peered down at it, looked exactly like a boxing glove.

From the doorway of his apartment, Frank Riley watched the movers carry the last of the Hogensons' furniture downstairs. He was bone-tired.

It had been quite an evening! First, Faye had refused to believe that Donald was really Donald, because he was not the small boy she remembered. She decided he must be the man from the pest-control company, and she insisted on leading him into the kitchen to show him the many cracks and holes through which pesky insects came and went. "Stamp!" she commanded him. "Stamp!" Seizing his elbows, she began a peculiar, bouncing dance with him until roaches scampered across the floor. "See?" she said. "I *told* you!"

Later, when the moving men lumbered past with steamer trunks on their shoulders, she was swept away by a recollection so far in the past that Frank had trouble remembering what year it had been. Once, long ago, they had taken a cruise.

"The love boat to Cuba!" Faye exclaimed. She stood in the doorway of her bedroom in sunglasses and a broad straw hat, a maraca clutched in each hand. "When do we leave?"

"Faye. No. It's not . . ."

"Shuffleboard! Pineapples filled with rum! Evening strolls in the moonlight!"

"Faye, we're not going anywhere."

Maracas clattered. Faye did a little stamping dance in her pom-pom slippers, spiraling slowly across the living room. "Romance, Frank. Romance!" She danced close to him, eyes half closed. So guileless was her expression, that despite all his fatigue and worry, he let her dance him around their living room to music that only she could hear.

That was how Muriel Hogenson found them when she arrived with the tray of medicine. She smiled. "Frank," she said, beckoning him out into the hall. "Frank?" Frank let Faye whirl from his arms and stepped outside.

"Muriel, don't go. Please don't."

"Oh, Frank, we got to, honey. We just got to. This isn't a home anymore, this place. It's the end of the world."

"I can't handle her, Muriel! Not on my own."

"You got to learn to do it. Here. Take these. This is a list of what and when. Inderal four times a day, after meals and at bedtime. Hydrodiuril twice a day, and so on. Okay?"

Frank nodded, squinting at the list. "Okay."

Sid appeared then, his cap already on, carrying the last of their bags. He was busily massaging his wrist. "Little arthritis, I think," he mumbled.

"That everything?" Muriel asked.

"That's it. Time to go. So long, Frank. Think about what I said. Out in Hoboken . . ."

"Yeah, Sid. Okay. I'll think about it."

Muriel was near tears. "Look after her, Frank. Look after yourself."

"You're not gonna see her? You're not gonna tell her . . ."

She shook her head. "I can't."

Frank shrugged. He tried to smile. "Well, it doesn't matter. Hell, she won't even know you're gone."

Muriel gave Frank a quick kiss, and then she and Sid went down the corridor, down the stairs, out to their son's car, out to Hoboken. Frank stood in his doorway watching. Neither of them looked back.

For a while after they had gone he continued to stand in the doorway, his hands full of bottles and pill boxes. He heard the truck pull away, heard Donald's car drive off. He heard the rumble of distant traffic. He caught a few unintelligible bars of a whistled song somewhere in the dark streets. He heard a tiny tapping from the vestibule, someone trying to repair the scrambled tile floor. "Harry," he said, nodding. "Harry never gives up."

But except for that small tapping, the building itself was still. There was no happy talk and laughter from the fourth floor, where Mason was now sole resident. Nor was there any music from the third floor, which Marisa now occupied all by herself.

Frank sighed and shuffled back into his apartment. Faye was not in the living room. The maracas and the straw hat lay on the couch. A fan of light spread under the door of the bathroom.

"Faye?"

"That you, Muriel?"

Frank distributed vials and potions along the top of the dresser. "Medicine time. Come on out, Faye, and let's do this."

"Where's Muriel? I want Muriel."

"I'm Muriel now. Are you coming out, or do I come in?"

"Hold it! I'm not dressed! Send Frank. Frank?"

"Yes?"

"Who's that?"

"It's Frank. I'm Frank, now."

"Oh. Okay. Come on in."

Frank opened the bathroom door to discover his wife, fully dressed, standing in the bathtub with the shower curtain wrapped around her.

"Put on the red record," she said.

"We don't have a red record."

"Muriel has a red record. She always puts it on when we take our medicine. Helps the pills go down."

"I guess she took it. I don't have it, Faye."

"Sing for me, then."

"Sing?"

"Sure! Come on, Frank. Sing one of the old songs. *You* know." She winked at him.

"Okay. Okay. I'll sing. You open your mouth. Say *frog*."

So, measuring Faye's medicine into a spoon, Frank sang a few bars of "Moonlight Serenade," and then a little bit of "Moonglow." Finally, he hummed the first of "The Anniversary Song," one of Faye's favorites. "Oh, how we danced on the night we were wed . . ."

Faye swallowed the medicine, then leaned forward and tenderly kissed him on the cheek. "Atta boy!" she said, propping up the corners of her mouth with her forefingers. "Smile! Look for that silver lining! Everything'll be all right. I'm gonna clean up that cafe, Frank. I'll clean it up right now." She started to climb out of the tub.

"Not now, baby. Sleep now." He led her to the bed.

"Okay. In the morning, then. Bobby'll help me. You'll see. Don't worry about a thing, okay?"

"Okay, honey. I won't worry." Patiently, Frank tucked her in and opened her window a crack. When he had turned out the light and was closing the door, she asked, "Did we miss the sunset?"

"Yeah. It was a little cloudy tonight. Tomorrow'll be better."

"Sure it will. 'Night, Frank."

"'Night, Faye."

He stood at the window in the living room without turning on any lights, looking down on what remained of their neighborhood. It was dark now. A dead zone.

He turned on a light and sank into his chair. He was too tired to do anything tonight, too tired even to board up the cafe against vandals. Why bother? They'd get in anyway. If they couldn't cut or smash their way in, they'd get keys from other vandals—vandals in three-piece suits. He was too tired to move. He leaned his head back on his comfortable old chair, and as he did so he looked at the coffee table.

There was the shattered and torn picture from the cafe, a picture of Faye and Frank and Bobby as they had been twenty years before, their arms around each other, all squinting into the spring sunlight, grinning in front of Rileys'. Beside it was the envelope from Carlos, the envelope containing the money that Mike O'Malley had refused to take. Also beside it was the brochure from Island Manor Retirement Village in Hoboken.

Frank picked up the folder and let it fall open on his lap. There were pictures of seniors watching television, playing crokinole and shuffleboard, dangling their legs on the edge of a swimming pool. All smiling. There were also pictures of the dining room, of the bright solarium, of the cheery bedrooms. Everything looked colorful and clean.

Frank's heart sank. He could picture them there. Easy. He could imagine the two of them imprisoned in those bright rooms, listening to strangers until they died.

It was only a matter of time.

"Only a matter of time," Frank murmured. He turned

his head so he could stare bleakly through the open window, over the dark hole where the neighborhood had been. And then, on the brink of a yawning gulf of sleep and despair, Frank Riley whispered into the night.

"Please," he said. "Somebody please help us."

He heard laughter far away. He heard someone passing in the street whistle a few bars of "Everything Old Is New Again." And then Frank Riley sank into a deep and hopeless sleep.

4 _____

"ONLY A MATTER of time . . ." Frank Riley had said, look-
ing down that darkening tunnel that, for him, was time.
Being human, Frank measured time in growth and decay,
the flourishing and waning of a tree, a building, a man.
Even in his dreams (troubling dreams that caused him to
say, "No, no," rolling his head on the back of his old
chair) he could not imagine time in any other way than
the relentless passage of years. For him, time was en-
tropy, the inexorable winding down of the cosmic clock.
Being human, he had only the span of a single life from
which to imagine time. Human, he had only five senses
through which to perceive reality. And, human, when he
fell asleep in his chair at the end of that day, he was
filled with black despair, except for whatever it was that
caused him to say, "Somebody, please help us."

Imagine, now, that his plea was answered.

Imagine that far away, in a part of another time that

was blending with Frank's as the fingers of two great hands might mesh, or as wisps of cloud might swirl together as they passed on separate journeys, something heard Frank Riley. Rather, it did not hear *him, for it lacked ears to hear; it* felt *him, felt the depth of his plea and the frail hope that he emitted, like a signal. Swerving, circling, it approached Frank Riley's little place in space and time, acquired the matter of Earth, assumed the spheroid shape of Earth, flattened itself to pass easily through unimaginable layers of space and time. Imagine that it became male, became female, and emerged at last through one of Earth's windows of need—the doomed building and the apartment where two old and vulnerable people slept . . .*

A small, spinning disk hovered over the ledge of Faye Riley's open window.

It was not much larger than two shallow bowls joined at the rims. Around the edge, dozens of lights gleamed like tiny jewels, and two oversized headlights shone at the front like yellow eyes. A rotor hummed in a cowling on its underside, and several delicate antennae and sensors bristled from a dome on its roof. It looked spiky, alert, and very dangerous.

Cautiously, whisker sensors testing the atmosphere, it skimmed over the sill and into Faye's room. Its lights swept the faded wallpaper, the old photographs in their frames, the albums and scrapbooks, the sticky medicine spoons on their plate. It spun when it passed the open door, and it hovered a moment, contemplating Frank Riley snoring in his armchair in the living room, and then it turned again and drifted over to the bed where Faye slept. The headlights played gently over her wrinkled throat and cheeks, over her frail white hair, over her eyes. The tone of its humming softened as it drew close.

What Faye heard in her sleep was the soft droning of bees, and the sound caused her to dream of an August holiday on a farm in Vermont, long ago. What she felt against her cheek was the soft touch of a tiny sensor, the slimmest filament, that reached out from under the saucer's edge.

Faye squinted, smiled, murmured. She brushed her hand across her face, and the saucer swerved aside, wobbling. For a moment it hung, rocking gently, considering the sleeping woman, then it passed into the living room and drifted close enough to Frank to be caught and wafted backwards by a violent snore. Again it approached, its headlights playing over him, the frail filament cautiously reaching toward his cheek, and again it was shaken by turbulence. This time it went on to explore the rest of the apartment. As it passed through the kitchen it suddenly dipped, zooming in diminishing circles above the counter, homing in finally on the electrical outlet. Its humming suddenly increased to a whine punctuated by tiny buzzes and blips, like exclamations of joy. Its headlights brightened. More beady lights twinkled and flashed on its perimeter. The whole rotund little body suddenly glowed, loosing a roseate aura.

Swooping back to the window ledge in the living room and perching there, riding the air currents drifting in and out of the room, it rolled its headlamps in a way that sent beams corkscrewing joyfully into the darkness.

Immediately it was answered by a flash in the haze above the city, and a moment later a second craft materialized, headed for the windowsill. This one was plumper, rounder, less angular than the first, and less bristly with antennae and sensors. Its headlamps protruded slightly into lidded orbs, and its tiered superstructure curved to fit its rounded top. It looked somehow more *feminine* than the first.

Down it came, this second small saucer, angling over the heaps of rubble, over the sign announcing Lacey Plaza, over the quiet cranes, trucks, and bulldozers.

But clearly something was wrong. Very wrong. The first little ship had approached cautiously but alertly, in control, ready to race away at the first alarm, but the second was clearly not in control. Its lights flickered and crossed, its flight path was a desperate wobble. Its humming was intermittent; in fact, it gasped. It was worn out, depleted, zonked.

From the ledge the first ship squeaked encouragement and hoisted the sash high, so that the new arrival could sweep straight through and into the living room. Down and in it came, its belly scuffing the sill, its edge knocking against the frame, spinning perilously close to Frank's lap. It recovered and struggled on, across the living room, down the hall, and into the kitchen. Its mate swooped ahead, beeping frantically.

Lower and lower—by the time it approached the counter, it was skimming the floor. Its whine rose to a desperate crescendo. Its dimming lights wavered. Finally, it skidded across the linoleum to the base of the cupboards, bounced off, and lay still. Its mate buzzed over it, emitting anguished beeps.

For a moment the little craft on the floor lay still. Light pulsed from its underbelly, like a weak strobe. Then it began to utter sounds again, first a whine, then a rattle, then a determined growl. It rose unsteadily, past the door handles, past the cupboard doors, almost to the edge of the counter. But before it reached the top, it slowed, and stopped, and began to sink again. Desperately it twisted. A small hatch on its flank popped open. Out soared a tiny silver grappling hook on the end of a gleaming filament. It arced up and across the counter into the slot of the toaster, and clamped there. Doggedly, the little machine hauled itself over the edge and then across to the outlet. From another hatch emerged a gleaming plug at the end of a silver arm. Up and out it stretched, rearing back like a cobra. It plunged into the socket.

The effect was immediate and wonderful.

The little ship trembled. It hummed. Its lights began to glow again. In three minutes the plug detached. The extension arm zipped back inside and the hatch snapped shut. The ship sprang off the counter and dove through a dazzling series of rolls and figure eights above the stove. Then it zoomed into the dining room in search of its mate, and found a faded nightie floating in Faye's doorway. The other little ship was tucked underneath, lights glowing through the sheer fabric. Around the living room he drifted like a ghost, clicking gleefully. He circled Frank, wriggled, and was about to drift out the window when he was stopped short by his mate.

A pair of extension arms had sprouted from her smooth sides, and on the ends were pincerlike claws. Chattering, scolding, she snatched the nightgown away and pointed at the smashed picture on the coffee table.

A brisk exchange followed. Together they swooped to examine this wreckage, one of them gathering the pieces of broken glass, the other reaching out a pincer to touch the rips in the photograph. They turned to face each other, bobbed, and then moved with blurring speed.

In seconds the rips in the old picture vanished, together with the yellow stains of age, and there it was, glossy and new, as if the picture of the three Rileys had been taken only yesterday. Seconds more and the broken frame was repaired, its cracked and blackened varnish replaced with lustrous oil. Even the broken glass was magically restored —nonglare!

The operation was fast but noisy. There were rattlings, hisses, hammerings, and clicks, and although none of these was as loud as Frank's snores, they were enough to awaken Faye. She was not alarmed. Nothing alarmed Faye anymore. Nothing had alarmed her for many years. She was curious, that was all.

And so, knotting the cord of her dressing gown, she was not surprised to see her nightie lying in a heap on the floor. Nor was she surprised, standing in the doorway of her bedroom, to see two flying saucers hovering over the coffee table, one shiny and angular, the other round and plump.

She waved. "Hi there," she said.

Beeping alarm, they swooped into the hall and vanished. Faye came forward, feeling the air where they had been. Very gently she took Frank's horn-rimmed glasses off his nose and put them on. More gently still, she picked up the picture, now gleaming and spotless, just the way it had been twenty years before when she had had it framed. She nodded. Yes, there she was, in her apron, a wooden stirring spoon still in her hand. And there was Frank in his apron, wearing his crooked grin, raising half a cup of coffee to the photographer. And there was Bobby with his arm around her.

"Bobby," she said.

And there was the cafe, clean and shiny, the way they always tried to keep it. "You see?" she whispered to her sleeping husband. "I *told* you I'd clean it up!" And she kissed him gently on the forehead.

At that moment there was a metallic thump in the kitchen, and then another and another. She looked. Her toaster, drawn by its cord by the male saucer, was proceeding down the hall and up the stairs to the roof. The other saucer hovered a little behind, turning to regard Faye with large and luminous eyes.

"Me?" Faye touched her chest. "You want me to come with you? Sure!" Smiling, she followed her visitors down the hall and up the stairs, out onto the roof in the summer night.

The roof of 817 East Ninth Street was like most other roofs on old buildings in the neighborhood—flat and dirty. A four-foot brick parapet closed it in. Years ago, during the thirties and forties, the women of the building used to go there to sunbathe and gossip on summer afternoons, and a few of the old wooden chaises they had used were still there, gray and rotten now. When Bobby was twelve, he had kept homing pigeons in a little coop Frank had helped him build beside the chimney, and it was still there as well, rickety and rusty.

The saucers headed straight for this coop, with the old toaster bumping along behind.

"Let me get that door for you," Faye said, hurrying past when she saw where they were going. "Latch is a bit tricky. Sticks."

She unhooked it and held it open, and the saucers drifted through, turning this way and that, inspecting. There was an excited interchange of beeps when they discovered the old metal barrel that Bobby had laid on its side for extra shelter, and even more excitement when they spied the collection of junk that Frank had tossed into a corner by the chimney over the years, thinking he might someday use it. There were old bicycle parts and motorcycle parts, old car parts and pieces of restaurant equipment that had long since been replaced.

When the saucers swooped out for a closer inspection of

this junk, Faye stuck her head inside the coop. "It's a mess! A real mess! If you folks are moving in, how 'bout I get my broom and clean it up a bit?"

Leaving the door ajar, she started back towards the stairs, but before she had taken five steps the saucers had zipped back inside and done their own cleanup. Just as they had repaired the smashed photograph, they worked so fast that their movements blurred into a single point of swirling light, like a child's sparkler on the Fourth of July. The refuse of years vanished. The cedar flooring gleamed golden brown, like new. Even the nailheads shone. In another instant, another blur, and the whole coop was exactly the way it had been when Bobby and Frank had finished it. Even the hutches were back again with the names of birds over their entrances, and although Faye couldn't read them from where she stood, she could, to her great delight, suddenly remember them: "Studebaker!" she said, pointing. "Kaiser! Hudson! Edsel!" She laughed and opened her hands to the clear sky as if she expected the white wings to come spiraling down as she had seen them on so many nights like this one, waiting with Bobby. "You're *fixers,* aren't you?" she said to the saucers.

But the saucers ignored her. They had dragged the old toaster into the overturned drum in the coop, and were busy demolishing it. Faye moved close. Yes, they were taking it apart! They had already discarded the cord and the plastic handles. The rubber feet followed. As Faye watched in wonder, they cut the metal body of the toaster into thin strips and drew these into their bodies by some means that she could not see. Bit by bit, all the metal parts of the toaster vanished.

Seconds later, with a crackle like lightning ripping across a summer sky, shards of hot white light exploded out of the drum, through the slats of the pigeon coop. It lit the entire roof. It even lit the sky.

"Fireworks!" Faye exclaimed, clapping. "Oh wonderful! I love fireworks!"

_____

5

HARRY AWOKE IN his basement bedroom to find his door
open and his floor swept clean. He sat up, gaping.

There were his boxing trophies neatly arranged on their
shelves, even the ones that Poncho had smashed against the
walls. There was his TV set, like new. And there were all
his toys and models restored, even the ones that Ramirez
had kicked to pieces. In fact, one space-station model now
bore features and details that it never had before. Harry
reached out and touched it with the finger of one huge
hand; a solar vane waved gently to him.

Suddenly, Harry wanted to see something. Still in his
pajamas, he hurried out and upstairs to the vestibule, where
he had labored so futilely the night before.

The tile floor gleamed like new, with the number 817
resplendent in the center. Lost in wonder, Harry sank to his
knees and spread his big hands on the cool, clean, beautiful
surface.

* * *

In apartment 3C, two floors above, Marisa woke up and looked for her plaster statue of St. Anthony standing on his little table behind the door. Every morning, that was the first thing she looked for. In fact, she had placed the little table in that spot so she could see the statue anytime, from any point in her apartment. He reminded her of Hector and his promise to come safely back to her. So, this morning was no different, except . . . except that it *was* different!

Marisa sat up suddenly. Heartbroken, hadn't she cried herself to sleep the night before because Carlos had smashed her statue? Hadn't she left all the fragments scattered on the floor? So, *where were they?*

Marisa got up and looked. Someone had cleaned up the mess. Every fragment. Not even dust was left. But who had done this? Where were the pieces?

She looked in the wastebasket. Nothing. She tiptoed into the kitchen and checked the garbage under the sink. Nothing. She opened the closet door. Nothing. Impulsively she opened the fridge, and staggered back, hands to her mouth. There was her statue, fully restored! Perfect! Right beside the milk.

Wide-eyed, Marisa Esquivel murmured a little prayer.

In apartment 4C, Mason Baylor woke up with no hangover. Even before he opened his eyes he knew he had no hangover, and he did not believe it, because he remembered that after knocking over his easel and throwing all his paintings out the window, he had finished all the beer in his refrigerator, and there had been quite a lot.

Cautiously he opened one eye, then the other. He felt fine. Even more cautiously, he sat up. He still felt fine. But there was something that was not right; rather, something was *too* right. He looked around. It was . . . it was that the studio was *tidy*. His easel, which he had kicked over in his frustration the night before, was standing where it always did, with his paintbox and palette beside it. His brushes had been freshly cleaned. His paints, hurled into the four corners of the room the night before, were now perfectly arranged in the colors of the spectrum. Even the various articles of clothing that he normally left strewn about were hung up in his closet. Most astonishing, the door that Carlos had kicked out had been repaired, and the broken bits of wood cleaned up.

"Wait a minute," Mason said, standing up. "Wait a *minute!*"

Only the canvasses that he had thrown through the window were still missing. He remembered them, all his work, spinning away like boomerangs as he had pitched them out one after the other. He remembered them scattered and broken in the street, in the adjoining lot. But when he opened the window wide and leaned out, there was no sign of them. All had vanished.

Mason tiptoed across the room. Warily, he opened the door on hinges that no longer squeaked. He said into the empty hallway, "What *is* this?"

Down on the second floor, Frank Riley was grumpy. He had not slept well in his armchair, and he was not looking forward to going down into the wreck of his cafe. Also, Faye was being difficult. She kept prattling about flying saucers as he was getting her dressed.

"Two of them, Frank. This big."

"Right. Two of them."

"They *must* have come in through the window."

"Lift your foot, honey, so I can put this shoe on."

"And you didn't even wake up, even when they were

flying right around your head. I should have waked you up."

"No, dear."

Many times in recent years she had wakened him, full of excitement about something that needed talking about right then. Sometimes it would be an event from their past, some holiday with Bobby, or some romantic moment shared before Bobby was born. Sometimes it would be something far back in her girlhood, from the time when there were horses and awnings on East Ninth Street, and large-bellied jolly men stood in shady doorways, smoking cigars. Or, sometimes what Faye excitedly woke him up to tell him was something from a world that Frank Riley could never share—like the time a chorus line of birch trees danced through their apartment, or the night she was borne away by a large white swan, laughing, calling back to her husband to fly faster, faster...

"Lift your arms, Faye. Onnn it goes! Turn around, now. Let me zip it up."

"Anyway, there were two of them. Two *flying saucers*. And they were *different*. From each other, I mean. One was male and one was female."

"That's great Faye. Ma and Pa. Just like us."

"Yes," she beamed. "Just like us! And maybe, just like us, they'll have..."

"You gonna do your hair, honey, or do you want me to?"

"I can do it."

"Sure?"

"Sure. Really."

"Okay. I'll go make breakfast."

She raised her voice so he could hear her from the bedroom. "Anyway, Frank, it was the most wonderful thing.

You know that picture of us, of the three of us, that got smashed yesterday?"

"Mmm."

"Frank?"

"Yeah. I'm listening, honey."

"Well, they fixed it, Frank. Good as new. It's right there on the table."

"Faye, where's the toaster?"

"The what?"

"The toaster."

"On the roof. In the pigeon coop."

Frank leaned his elbows on the counter and put his face in his hands.

"They took it up there."

"The flying saucers did?"

"Um-hm. You can go up and look at it, but there isn't much left."

"Faye, could you tell me please why two small flying saucers should take our toaster into a pigeon coop?"

"Well, I thought maybe to fix it."

"Fix it."

"Sure, just the way they fix other things. You know very well, Frank, that toaster only works on one side. Has for years. But then, they ate it."

"Ate it."

She nodded.

His hand shaking slightly, Frank poured orange juice and began to make coffee. Soon Faye came out and joined him in the kitchen, sitting down quietly at the place he had set for her at the end of the table. Her white hair was neatly brushed, and she was smiling radiantly, in the way that had always, in all the years he had loved her, made him feel better. When he brought her coffee, he leaned over and kissed her lightly on top of her head.

She picked up her plate, looked thoughtfully at it, over-turned it, and threw it across the room, where it shattered to smithereens against the wall.

"Faye . . ."

"Like that," she said. "That was just what they looked like, only they had lights, and little things sticking out, and . . ."

"Faye, you just smashed a plate. You just put a dent in the wall."

"Don't *worry,* Frank. They're *fixers!*" She took the saucer from under her cup and tossed it across the room as well.

"Faye. Faye. Drink your orange juice, honey. I'll be right back."

Frank shuffled into the living room and sagged into his chair. Without Muriel's help he could not cope. He saw that. Every moment would have to be spent with Faye, looking after her, preventing her from destroying things, or from hurting herself.

Bitterly, he picked up Lacey's envelope of money in one hand and the brochure for Island Manor Retirement Village in the other. He patted his pockets for his glasses, failed to find them, and took Faye's rimless spectacles from the coffee table. Through them he peered at the number on the brochure, and then he picked up the phone and dialed.

He was beaten. He knew it.

But then, as he dialed the last digit, he saw the photograph on the mantel.

Like new.

A warm and soothing voice began to say into his ear, "Island Manor Retirement Village . . . Hello, Island Manor Retirement Village . . ." but Frank was oblivious to it, setting the phone back into its cradle, tottering across the living room like a man under a spell. He took the picture in both hands, staring at the happy faces looking out at him. He hurried back to the kitchen. "Faye!"

But she was gone and the apartment door was open. "Oh no!" He left the picture on the table and ran after her, only to bump into an immense human mass coming up the stairs.

"Harry! Have you seen Faye?"

The big man solemnly shook his head.

Then Frank heard her talking to somebody on the floor above, laughing gaily, like a girl again. In a minute he got to the third floor and found Mason Baylor and Marisa waiting for him. They all started to talk together.

"My statue . . ."

"My door . . ."

"My wife!"

Mason pointed. "Up on the roof. She said something about feeding time."

Frank was already heading towards the fourth floor, and then up the last flight of stairs, to the roof. The door stood open, and morning sun streamed down the stairwell.

Faye was at the old pigeon coop. She was a serene figure. Fingers of morning breeze plucked at the sleeves of her dress and played in her wispy hair. She was carrying an old muffin tin that Frank kept in the kitchen cupboard for scraps of this and that—nuts and bolts, odd nails and screws, an assortment of washers and extra parts—and as she drew close to the open door of the coop, she began to scatter these metal bits inside, close to the rusty oil drum lying on its side. She made soft buzzing sounds, as if summoning bumblebees and hummingbirds.

"Faye! Faye, honey!" Frank was breathless, but Faye seemed sublimely above all human frailty now, a white, drifting figure.

"I'm feeding them, Frank. They *need* this."

"Faye . . ." He turned back to Mason and Marisa, who had followed him upstairs, and to Harry, so large that he loomed above the skyline. "Our son, you know, he kept birds here a long time ago. Pigeons. Faye, c'mon now, okay. They aren't here anymore. All gone. Come on back. Finish your breakfast."

"Hey!" Mason said, squatting down to peer inside the drum. "What's that?"

Still clutching her statue, Marisa also bent down and peered into the drum. "That's mine!" she whispered to Mason.

"Tell him," Mason said. "He oughta know."

"Tell me what?"

"Well, Mr. Riley, that's my frying pan in there. I know because I just bought it last week. From Sears. Teflon. Has that special handle."

"Oh no." Frank pressed a hand to his mouth.

"More," Mason said. "That's my coffeepot in there. See? Sunbeam. You can see the 'Sun' on the top."

"Yeah," Harry said, also bending close. "And there's one of my trophies. The one I got in . . . in . . ."

"Oh, Faye!" Frank's voice was stricken. "Faye!" She did not answer him. She buzzed and hummed sweetly, scattering nuts and bolts. He grabbed her arm, spilling the contents of the muffin tray. "Faye, did you go in these people's apartments?"

"No, Frank! *They* did!"

"Who?"

"Them. In there."

"Faye, there's nobody in there, you understand that? There's nothin' in there but a toaster, a frypan, a coffeepot, and Harry's trophy. All of which, Faye, you took without permission."

"I did not!"

"Faye, listen to me, honey. Listen, please." Frank took both of her frail hands in his. "I need you here with me. I *need* you!"

"I'm here, Papa."

"We gotta tell the *truth,* you understand? Even if it hurts, we gotta tell things like they are."

"What do you *think* I'm doing!"

"Look, Mr. Riley, there's no harm done. Honest." Mason started into the pigeon coop. "I'll just take my pot back . . ."

"Yeah," Marisa said. "There's lotsa ways those things coulda gotten up here. Lotsa ways." She shrugged doubtfully. "Like, maybe, rats?"

"Hold it!" Faye said to Mason, who was already on his knees, reaching into the barrel. "They like . . ."

The pigeon coop exploded.

Something clanged inside the barrel, and lightning crackled in all directions through the chicken wire. Mason Baylor, hair and beard electrified, skidded out on his belly and lay still at Harry's feet.

". . . their privacy," Faye concluded. "That's what they like."

"Whazzit?" Mason struggled to his hands and knees.

"I know what it wasn't," Marisa said softly, backing up. "It wasn't any rat."

"I *told* you," Faye said. "Now shoo! Back off!" And with little brushing gestures she herded them all to the stairway, including the disheveled, befuddled Mason.

"Neutral corner," Harry murmured.

"Now give me *that.*" From Frank's pocket she snatched his gold watch, dropped it onto the asphalt roof, and crushed it with a brick.

"That was my father's!" Frank said, spreading helpless hands to Harry. "My *grandfather's!*"

Faye tossed the mangled timepiece into the coop, where it skidded to within a yard of the barrel. "Now watch!" she commanded and stepped back with her arms folded.

They watched.

For a moment, nothing, and then from the barrel came concerned buzzings and hums closely followed by the saucers themselves, peering out of the shadows.

"See?" Faye said. "There's Pa. There's Ma."

Fully charged and motors humming, the saucers warily approached the crushed watch and hovered over it, assessing the damage. From various hatches they extended tiny arms tipped by pincers, pliers, screwdrivers, and a variety of other devices. The humans scarcely had time to react before the saucers went to work, before everything blurred.

In milliseconds the watch was repaired. Smashed crystal, twisted arms, bent case, delicate spinning cogs—all as good as new. Even the time was right: 8:16.

"You see?" Faye said. "They're fixers!"

The saucers hovered placidly above their handiwork, gazing levelly at the astonished humans.

Harry leaned over and whispered in Mason's ear, "Do you see what I see?"

Mason stammered, groping for a reply. No words came.

Marisa clutched the plaster saint to her breast and uttered a quiet, wide-eyed prayer.

Finally, swallowing hard, Frank advanced. The saucers' buzzing grew hostile as he approached, and rows of lights around their rims blinked rapidly. Six feet away, he stopped and extended his hand, palm up.

The saucers hung, regarding him.

He looked back at Faye. "Wh . . . what do I say?"

"Nothing. You won't have to say anything, Papa."

She was right again, for soon the rounder and plumper of the two saucers swooped down, seized the end of the chain, and dropped the refurbished watch into Frank's out-stretched hand, while the other saucer turned in a bobbing circle, like a dance, and popped back into the oil barrel.

"It's *warm,*" Frank said, holding the watch in both hands. "The picture, the watch, the statue . . ." Eyes bulging, he turned suddenly and hurried off downstairs. The others followed.

They headed straight to the ground floor, to the cafe.

Rileys' was spectacular. The oak paneling glowed with fresh oil. The reflections from new fixtures glittered on the ceiling. Trimmed with maroon leatherette, the counter stools stood on gleaming chrome pedestals, and the counter itself awaited customers, every sugar canister and napkin box in its little aluminum rack. Behind the counter, the kitchen was ready. The grill was fixed, the coffee urns waited to be switched on, and the glass shelves—the ones that Carlos had smashed—were spotless, ready for the cakes and pies that had helped make Rileys' famous. Gone was the chipped arborite on the old tables. Gone were the creaky chairs and the old linoleum. The little dance floor near the jukebox lay ready for celebrating, dance-wax freshly sprinkled, and the jukebox itself glowed with rich color in all its many tubes and arches, holding records ready in mechanical fingers. All the photographs were back in their places on the walls, as good as new. Even the front windows had been replaced, so clean it would have been easy to walk right through them, had not the large, black-edged gilt letters been replaced as well: RILEYS' CAFE. The crazed and checkered varnish on the doors and outside wood had been cleaned away to reveal the rich wood underneath. Everything smelled new! The front door stood open, and beyond it, on the bright concrete step, lay a large mat saying WELCOME.

"You see!" Faye spread her arms. She was a young and radiant woman once again, as full of life as the cafe. "You *see?*"

Frank laughed incredulously, making astonished exclamations as he discovered new wonders. And then, Faye touched buttons on the glittering Wurlitzer and it magically responded to her touch, selected a record, turned it, and set its needle on the spinning disc. The rich and beautiful tones of Glenn Miller's "Moonlight Serenade" filled the room, and as Faye came towards him with her arms outstretched, Frank had to turn away for a moment and clean his glasses so he could see properly. And then, smiling, he held her, his left hand extended, holding her right, his other pressed against her back, and they began to dance to the slow music of that other time, gliding softly and effortlessly on the sprinkled floor. She laid her cheek against his. She closed her eyes. Without looking, she beckoned to Mason and Marisa where they stood near the counter, staring. "C'mon, you kids," she said. "Let's *all* dance!"

That morning the whole building looked different.

Nobody could tell *how*, exactly; but Gus, the bulldozer driver, rattling by in his pickup on his way to work, knew that somehow it had been improved overnight. He stopped and rolled down his window for a better look. "Hey," he said to Sammy, the foreman, when he got to the construction trailer. "What *is* it about that place?"

And the foreman took off his white hard hat and rubbed his bald head, and said, "I dunno. I *dunno*. I been wonderin' that myself. Looks . . . looks more solid, don't it?"

Later, the limousine with smoked windows pulled into the curb outside 817 East Ninth. None of the residents saw it. Mason was on the phone, Faye was giving Marisa a jitterbugging lesson, Harry was doing a little happy dancing of his own in one corner of the floor, and Frank was busy at a grill that was hotter and cleaner than it had been for many years, cooking a huge breakfast for everyone.

In the back seat, Nelson Kovacs's touched a button, which caused his window to glide down. He listened to the festive sounds spilling out of Rileys' Cafe—all the laughter and the big-band swing. He examined the front of the building, which looked better than he had ever seen it.

The lower lid of Nelson Kovacs's left eye twitched. He thought of his daughter in the very expensive French school, and of his son, who was almost a Harvard MBA. He thought of his very large mortgage. He thought of the quizzical way Mr. Lacey looked at him whenever they discussed this wretched building.

"Drive on," he said.

As the limo rolled away, he picked a telephone off its cradle and punched buttons. His call would wake up Carlos Chavez. It would be very brief, very terse and pointed. He would remind Carlos of the handsome fee he had been paid, and he would ask him why those tenants were still there—not only still there, but *celebrating!*

He would tell him to get his job done.

Now.

6 _____

ALL MORNING, HARRY waited on the roof, keeping a respectful distance from the old pigeon coop. For long periods he didn't see much of anything, except the rusted barrel overturned inside. But every now and then one of the saucers would emerge and regard him with large and softly glowing eyes.

Once, after they had gazed at each other for a long time in silence, Pa saucer timidly drifted out of the barrel, out of the coop, and came half the distance towards Harry. Different sensors emerged from his superstructure and turned towards the man. He hovered; then, as gently as he had emerged, he drifted back into the coop, facing Harry all the time.

Meanwhile, in the cafe, Mason was on the phone. Frank, Faye, and Marisa exchanged opinions on what the saucers were and what they meant. For Faye, things were perfectly clear. "Fixers," she said, shrugging. "Simple as that. Come to help us."

Marisa agreed. "A miracle, that's what's happening. I think we should just leave it alone, be thankful, let it happen."

Frank nodded. For years, powerless to stop it, Frank had watched the subtle deterioration of his neighborhood. He had seen his business decline; he had watched old friends give up, shake their heads, board up their shops; he had watched gangs move in, move through, like sand shifting. Sometimes in the night he heard screams where there had once been laughter. For months he had watched glumly as the other residents of 817 East Ninth moved out, leaving their apartments vacant—the Grandeys, the Moscowitzes, the Tatums, and now the Hogensons. For years he had watched his beloved Faye withdraw into worlds where he could not follow. It had been so long since he had hoped that he had almost forgotten what hope was.

But now, the saucers had changed all that. Overnight they had lifted him out of the depths. They had magically given him back his cafe and made Faye joyful. What more could he ask? As he cooked up a breakfast on the spotless grill, he whistled. He sang bits of songs from the fifties. He even did a little dance, spatula held high.

"Zapped!" Mason was saying into the telephone. "It felt like a thousand volts. It felt like *ten* thousand volts."

"I warned him, didn't I?" Faye touched Marisa's arm. "He just barged in."

Marisa nodded. She turned back to listen to Mason on the phone.

"So, you guys wanna tell me what's goin' on? You got some kinda experimental aircraft, right? Programmed to high voltage, right? What? I *told* you. They're in the pigeon coop! On the roof!"

Frank shook his head. He flipped eggs on the grill. "Don't give 'em your name," he said.

"I *tried* the Army. They said to call you guys. Look, I'll make a deal. You tell me what they are, and I'll tell you where to find them."

Faye sighed.

"They aren't *weapons*, Mason," Marisa said. "Weapons destroy, they don't build."

But he was shouting now, waving his free arm. "I know you guys! You develop all these devices, all these weapons, robots, and autogyros and smart bombs, and then when they get away from you, *you don't know anything!* You guys are a *menace,* that's what I think! Why should we worry about the Russians when we got *you?* What? Whatd'ya mean, abusive? I'm a citizen! I've got a right to know . . ."

Faye smiled sadly and patted Marisa's arm again. She winked. "Men. They can be so silly. *We* know why they've come, don't we dear."

Marisa looked at her, wide-eyed. "I listened to the news," she said. "There wasn't anything about them. Do you think . . . do you think that maybe they're just . . . for *us?*"

Faye winked again.

Mason was shouting louder now, and pounding the doorframe. "What do you mean, *medical assistance?* No! No, I am not high on something. I don't take drugs, I'm not drunk, I'm perfectly sane, and *I tell you that there are two little flying saucers* . . . All right! All right, I *will* call the police!" He slammed down the phone. "Can you *believe* those guys!"

Frank served fried eggs onto plates. "Whatd'ya expect?" he asked, spreading his arms. "You sounded like a nut!"

Marisa nodded solemnly. "I wouldn't believe you. I'd think you were reading too many comic books. Having funny dreams, maybe."

"What if they're dangerous? What if they zap us all like they zapped me?"

"Uh-unh," Marisa said, shaking her head.

Frank brought plates out and laid them on the table. "Thing is, Mason, they didn't come after you. *You* went after *them!* You crawled into that barrel, remember. Could be you were asking for it."

"You people *believe* this, don't you! You really believe that those things up on the roof . . ."

Frank chuckled and patted his shoulder. "Relax, Mason. Eat eggs. Faye, could you get the coffee, please?"

"Sure."

Still smiling, Frank watched her go. How great to see her doing things again! Taking hold. Living in reality. Watching Faye move through that cafe, Frank nodded. Yeah, he did believe. He knew exactly why those saucers had come. He took a big, contented bite of breakfast.

In the kitchen, Faye happily poured coffee for them all.

How wonderful it was to have people around again! Laughing, and discussing, and arguing, just like old times. Why, sometimes in the old days, the discussions in the cafe used to go on till two, three in the morning. Frank would pull down the blinds. Sometimes he would cook and sometimes she would, depending who was busier talking. Old friends like Mike O'Malley would rap on the door and come in for coffee and a bite to eat. Sometimes they would talk politics, and sometimes sports, and sometimes the raising of children, and sometimes everything together in a boisterous jumble. But no matter what they talked about, or no matter how heated the discussions became, they would part friends. Always. They were friends for all those years.

And then . . . and then . . .

Faye was not sure what had happened then. When she tried to remember, she was just not sure.

A silver shape twinkling with lights whizzed past her, circled once, and dropped into the sink, among the broken eggshells Frank had left.

Faye drew close. The saucer's top bristled with antennae. From underneath came a spurt of scratching and hisses, and then, as briskly as he had come, the saucer lifted and hummed away back into the hall, leaving in the sink five perfectly repaired, empty eggshells. Wonderingly, Faye picked them out one at a time and set them in egg cups. "Thank you!" she called. "We'll keep them till Easter! We'll paint them, Bobby and me."

Suddenly the saucer swooped back like a busy man who had forgotten something, hovered near Faye's 1940s breadbox, reached out with his pincers to open the lid and remove the cellophane-wrapped loaf inside, and then ducked in and lifted off.

Busy setting the eggs in egg-cups, Faye saw nothing of this. "Pa?" she said, turning around, looking for the little saucer. "Hey, Pa. Where are you?"

Mason looked in from the cafe just in time to glimpse the breadbox sailing away. His eyes widened. He laughed a high-pitched and uncomfortable laugh. Without moving his head he said to Marisa and Frank, "Did either of you see that?"

"No."

"What?"

"A breadbox just flew through the door, into the hall."

"A breadbox."

"Yes. *Yes,* dammit! Don't look at me like that!"

They hurried out into the corridor. The light was dim, but bright enough to see the breadbox bumping erratically from wall to wall, headed for the stairwell.

Ahead, Ma saucer rose in a graceful spiral up the stairwell with one of Harry's boxing trophies dangling beneath her. Harry himself came up from the basement, laughing and slapping his knees. "You shoulda *seen* her! You shoulda seen that saucer watchin' *television*. I never seen . . ." He halted at the sight of the free-floating breadbox. He thumped the heel of his hand against his temple, shook his head, looked again.

"Wait for me!" Faye said, hurrying out of the kitchen after the others.

Inside the box, Pa saucer was badly disoriented. He caromed off a wall, bounced against a railing, narrowly missed crashing into the banister, and finally skidded to a halt on the landing.

The box's lid opened a slit. Two yellow orbs glowed in the darkness.

The humans edged closer.

"Don't touch it!" Mason warned. "Don't go near it!"

Frank brushed him away. "I'm gonna speak to it," he whispered.

Marisa touched his arm. "Be *careful*."

"Hello in there," Frank said. He waved. "Hi!"

The glowing orbs regarded him steadily out of the darkness.

"I just want to say thanks. Thanks for what you've done."

A metallic arm came forward. Metallic fingers lifted the lid an inch.

"You *see?*"

"He likes you," Faye said. "You don't have to say anything."

"Welcome to Earth! Welcome to America! We're peaceable people here . . ."

"That's right!" Mason said. "Lie to it!"

Frank shrugged, remembering the war, remembering all the wars since, remembering the highway carnage, the murders and beatings, remembering his savaged cafe.

Frank drew a deep breath. "Well, we do our best. Thing is, we don't want to hurt you. Honest. Anyway, I have a pretty good idea you guys can look after yourselves, right? Am I right?"

No response, except for a resonant, confident humming.

Ma saucer swooped down the stairwell. She circled the breadbox and then passed unconcernedly down the hall and into the cafe. A moment later the lights dimmed.

"Feeding time," Harry said, nodding. "Rechargeable powerplant. Batteries not required."

"Marisa," Frank said, "you try. Maybe they know Spanish."

She shook her head and drew back, frightened, but Frank brought her forward again. "C'mon. He won't hurt you."

"Okay," she said in Spanish. "Don't hurt anybody, okay, you in there?"

No answer.

"Okanjo kudahsai!" Mason said suddenly.

"What's *that?*" Faye asked.

"It's Japanese for 'May I have the check, please?' I just thought, well . . ." Mason shrugged. "I used to eat a lot of sushi . . ."

Suddenly, the lid slammed down and with much clanging from inside, the breadbox lifted straight up the stairwell and vanished.

"That's that," Mason said.

"C'mon," Faye said, tugging him by the sleeve. "Might

as well finish our breakfast. We can all sit down at the
table, just like a family. Okay, Harry?"

He nodded.

"Okay, Mason? Marisa?"

"Sure."

"Besides, Ma's back there, plugged in just like last
night. We should keep her company."

So together, just like a family, they started back down
the corridor.

Carrying his aluminum baseball bat, Carlos Chavez
took the steps of the entrance two at a time, shoved open
the door, and strode through the vestibule. He was not in a
good mood. After watching the Hogensons move out the
night before, he had gone uptown for a little celebrating,
certain that the other tenants would soon follow. "Only a
matter of time," he had told Kovacs. "Day or two, at most,
the place's yours."

But then he got the phone call.

Cursing, he found his baseball bat and ran to Rileys'
Cafe. He went alone. He didn't bother to use his key on the
front door—just rammed the bat through the glass and
freed the lock from inside. He paused. Something was different here. Something was weird! There were no loose
tiles. The floor gleamed like new. Along the corridor where
Poncho had scrawled lurid graffiti, everything was fresh
and clean—walls, woodwork, and floor. It even *smelled*
fresh.

"Painters!" Carlos snarled, slamming his bat into a pan-
eled door. "Cleaners! Fixers!"

And there were sounds, sounds coming from down the
hall, from the cafe. Sounds that fearful people should not
make.

Conversation. Laughter.

There was another sound also, a sound Carlos was hardly conscious of, but which caused him to brush an angry hand past his ear as he strode down the corridor. It was a faint but persistent drone. Like a wasp. Like a horse-fly. Like some sonic device, homing in on him.

Again Carlos brushed at the sound. He slammed his bat against the wall. He headed for the door of the cafe.

Inside, Faye was pouring fresh cups of coffee. Less than a yard away, Ma saucer perched on the counter, plugged into the wall socket. Lights winked in the flat gondola on her underside, and around her periphery. Brighter lights shone at the ends of telescoping lateral arms, which angled down to touch the counter. Glowing orbs swiveled from Frank and the rest of the watching group to Faye and back again.

The lights in the cafe flickered.

Frank edged close to the saucer and bent to eye level.

"Careful!" Mason warned.

"Could you tell me . . ." Frank began.

The glowing orbs changed from yellow to orange. Something buzzed deeply and ominously: a warning.

". . . tell me why you . . ."

The plug whipped out of the socket. The arm recoiled into the body of the saucer, and the door snapped shut. With a bearish snarl, Ma sprang straight up, hovered a split second, and then skimmed so close to Frank's head that his few remaining hairs fluttered in the breeze of her passage.

Marisa screamed. Mason pulled her down just as the saucer zipped overhead.

Ma snarled through the front door, and away.

"That's it!" Mason said, getting to his feet and helping Marisa up. "I'm calling the cops!"

But he did not get to the phone.

Carlos was suddenly there. Quick in his sneakers and

sweat suit, Carlos slipped through the doorway and blocked Mason's path. He gripped his aluminum bat in both hands. The tip of it traced menacing little figure eights at knee height. "You wanna call the cops, Picasso? C'mon." He jerked his head back towards the telephone. "Call the cops."

"Bobby! Bobby!" Faye's cup of coffee clattered to the counter. She ran to him.

"Back off! My name's not Bobby!" He waved his bat at Harry. "You! What's goin' on here?"

The big man shrugged. "Eatin' breakfast."

"You know what I mean! Who cleaned this place up? Who fixed it? Come on!"

No one answered. In the silence, the buzzing hum from outside in the hallway grew louder. Suddenly it became two sounds, two separate, outraged snarls.

"They did," Frank said.

An upside-down pot and a wastebasket sailed through the door in tight formation.

Carlos had no time to duck. The pot connected just above his temple, knocking him into a scrambled heap, and then, as he groped for his bat, groggily picking himself up and saying, "Who threw that? Whoever did it is *finished!* Hospitalized!", it executed a little pirouette and sailed back, hitting him on the other side. This time, before Carlos had time to retrieve his bat, the wastebasket dipped down and scooped it off the floor. Then, as suddenly as they had come, pot and wastebasket resumed formation and vanished.

Carlos staggered to his feet. "What the hell *is* this?"

Harry shrugged. Frank shrugged. The others shrugged.

Carlos was not used to humiliation. He was not used to being beaned by pots, or to having his tools whisked out of his hands. And he was not used to having people smile at his embarrassment, especially people he was supposed to be intimidating.

He smoothed his hair. He straightened his track suit. "You wait here! I got a lot more to say to you!" Still a bit unsteady on his feet, he chased after the can containing his stolen bat.

Everyone followed him to the roof except Faye, who stayed behind to cook a breakfast for Bobby.

"We should warn him," Mason whispered as they climbed.

Frank shrugged. "Why?"

"Well, you saw what happened to me."

"Exactly! So why should we warn Carlos?"

"They might kill him," Mason said.

When they reached the roof and Carlos approached the pigeon coop, Mason shouted over the metallic clatter that was coming from inside. "I wouldn't go over there if I were you. I wouldn't go anywhere near . . ."

Carlos whirled, snarling. "I thought I told you to stay where you were!"

"Don't touch anything!"

But already Carlos was grabbing for the handle of his bat, which was sticking out of the oil drum. When he seized it, the pigeon coop fell silent. All clatter ceased.

Carlos pulled.

Something pulled back.

Carlos clamped both hands on the bat handle, braced himself, and heaved.

Immediately there was a jerk in the opposite direction that yanked Carlos right off his feet and sent him sailing into the clutter of metal inside the coop.

Mason covered his face. Marisa gasped.

Then came the same high-voltage explosion that Mason had caused earlier, except that this time it was more violent. *Much* more. Lightning jabbed in all directions through the slats of the coop. Chicken wire glowed. Smoke rose from the wood. The pile of scrap shuddered from tremendous jolts of voltage deep inside. Pots fused. Plastic handles shriveled like cardboard. The baseball bat melted into an aluminum puddle.

Hair erect, mouth wide in a silent scream, electricity shooting from the end of every finger like freaky blue fingernails, Carlos was shaken like a rag doll and finally hurled backwards out of the coop.

He leaped up, ragged, burned, and wild-eyed. Large orange orbs regarded him out of the depths of the oil drum. Crablike pincers gathered the jewelry that had been snipped off him—his pendants, his rings, even his earring. Thin and unearthly laughter echoed inside the rusty drum.

Carlos howled. He ran. He screamed all the way down the four flights of stairs, taking them three at a time, and when he hit the street, he was still screaming.

The people on the roof leaned over the balustrade to watch him go, his track suit shredded like the costume of a fool.

Frank shrugged and turned to the pigeon coop. "Well, we tried to warn him, didn't we?"

A silver pincer reached out and seized the last of Carlos's pendants. It vanished. Inside the drum, something crunched.

A string of small marble beads clicked in Martin Lacey's fingers. He stared unblinkingly at Nelson Kovacs. Kovacs had been seized by a cramp in his right thigh and was hopping stiff-legged around the office, leaning on chair backs and whimpering pathetically.

"Zinc," Lacey said. "You have a zinc shortage. You should take zinc pills. You know, Kovacs, you should look after yourself better. *Mens sana in corpore sano.* Know what that means?"

Kovacs shook his head. He was biting his lip, beating the rock-hard leg muscle with both fists.

"'A sound mind in a healthy body.' Didn't you study Latin?"

Kovacs shook his head again. He went down on his hands and knees on Lacey's Persian carpet, stretching the leg like a runner in the starting blocks.

"You, a lawyer, didn't study Latin. Shameful. Look at you: twenty-five pounds overweight, sweat streaming from a little muscular discomfort. Tsk. You're probably a meat eater, right?"

Kovacs nodded.

"I thought so. Meat eaters, you know, work in bursts. They're fine for the short haul, but then they get sluggish, especially if they feed too well."

"Mr. Lacey..." Kovacs limped back to his chair and plunked down, mopping his brow. "Mr. Lacey, I swear that building..."

"Maybe you've been eating too well. Could that be the trouble?" The little beads clicked.

"There's something funny about that building. Something uncanny. How could they make those repairs so *fast?*"

The beads clicked.

"What do they have to *celebrate,* those people? Do you know, when I drove by there, they were dancing. *Dancing!*"

The beads clicked.

Kovacs's eye twitched under the sweat. "You know what I think? I think they've organized somehow. Maybe linked up with a union. Teamsters, maybe."

The beads stopped clicking. Martin Lacey frowned

under his silky gray hair. He touched a button on his desk. He said, "Number five salad, please." He turned back to Kovacs. "Another thing about meat eaters: they are easily distracted. They go after this, then that, then something else. Don't keep their eye on what they want, on what's really important. Do you understand what I'm saying, Mr. Kovacs?"

"Yes, sir."

"It's very important not to be distracted. Important to make rational decisions and follow through. Follow... through."

"Yes, sir."

"You remember, of course, our decision about this building. Same as the rest. Empty by June fifth."

"Yes, sir. I know, but..."

"Empty. Uninhabited. Void. Evacuated. Abandoned. So that it can, perfectly legally, be *removed.*"

The salad plate arrived. Lacey selected a stick of celery and munched slowly. "Chew well," he said, nodding at Kovacs.

"Sir, I know you don't want to be bothered with details..."

"You're right."

"... but I have to tell you, about the operatives..."

"Mr. Kovacs, you and I have *had* this conversation. I've told you, I want to know *nothing.*" Lacey's jaw muscles hardened. The celery crunched. He tossed the little string of beads on his desk. "Nothing. If you have to escalate, escalate! That's what I pay you for."

"There's some danger that..."

"Wrong. There is no danger, because I also pay you to keep me *out* of danger. Correct?"

"Yes, sir."

"And please look after yourself better. Eat celery. Take

zinc. And swim. Swimming is a great conditioner. Don't you have a pool at your place?"

"Yes, sir. But I just never have the time . . ."

"You should take time, Nelson. Take time to keep yourself in shape. Take time to spend with your children; otherwise, they'll grow up and be gone before you know it."

"My children *are* gone, Mr. Lacey. One is . . ."

Lacey held up his hands. "Please. I prefer not to know the details. The personal details. That way, I don't get too involved with my people. Emotionally involved. You know that."

"Yes, sir."

"It's much cleaner that way."

"Yes, sir. You always say that money is much cleaner than emotions."

"Exactly, Nelson. *Exactly.* Keep that in mind."

7 _____

IN THE DAYS that followed, the human inhabitants of 817
East Ninth and the nonhuman inhabitants arrived at tacit
agreements. All five humans understood, for example, that
no one should go closer than ten feet to the pigeon coop;
and although Harry spent many hours sitting in deep con-
templation with his back against the chimney, fifteen feet
away, the saucers unconcernedly came and went about
their business. On the other hand, the saucers did not in-
vade human spaces except when necessary to make repairs,
or to recharge, or to acquire raw material for wornout
parts.

"Live and let live," Harry said.

"Don't knock it," Mason replied. "It works."

Something was working. There were no recurrences of
the angry outbursts of the first day; there were no further
signs of Carlos; there were no further threats or bribes from
Lacey or Kovacs.

Once again, the cafe began to draw customers. At coffee breaks and lunchtimes, some of the workers came in from the construction sites. It was cool inside, and clean. Frank got up on his ladder and oiled the old ceiling fans. When he switched them on, they miraculously began to turn again, wafting fresh air in a slow and soothing breeze.

The old atmosphere returned. Sometimes large men in undershirts and hard hats who operated the heavy machinery would drop nickels into the jukebox and listen nostalgically to tunes they hadn't heard since they were kids. And sometimes when things were slow, Faye and Frank would dance a little on the polished floor, laughing together. Once a day all the residents would gather to drink coffee and to discuss the miracle that had befallen them, examining it from every angle.

And, indeed, it was a miracle. Not only had the saucers fixed the damage done by Carlos and the Crusaders, but also they continued to improve the old building in dozens of small ways. They refashioned chipped mouldings and broken cornices. They scoured the ancient pipes so hot water flowed abundantly again, with lots of pressure. Every day they vacuumed and polished the place sparkling clean, despite all the dust from the surrounding lots.

Just as they improved the building, so they also restored the inhabitants.

Harry, for example. Sometimes, leaving the pigeon coop or returning to it, one of the saucers would drift across to where the big man watched them, leaning against the chimney. It would hang in front of him, humming gently. Its glowing orbs would soften. Gazing into them, Harry would begin to smile. It had been a long time since he had smiled; a long time since he had felt anything but confusion and fear.

Ever since his last, disastrous foray into the ring, Harry

had felt broken, an object of ridicule. Sometimes he still heard mocking laughter, the same laughter that had seared his brain during that last fight when he had struggled to get up, and the ring had tipped and swayed, and the referee had counted over him. He believed he would hear that laughter forever. So he preferred toys and television to people: toys did not laugh. Television did not mock him. That was why, although he was still a powerful man, he had hidden when he heard Carlos coming with his gang.

But on the roof, alone with one or both of the hovering saucers, he found that he could smile again, that he was not afraid. He began to feel whole.

Mason Baylor also went through changes. Startling changes. For one thing, he knew his art would never be the same. Painting old buildings suddenly seemed less important. What mattered to him now was life and people, especially the people in 817 East Ninth, who had shared his strange experience. That jolt of electricity on the roof had broken his connection with what had gone before, but it had *made* a connection, also. And some of that magical current still tingled in him. He felt as if he were surfing, swept along by life, washed by spray and wind.

For another thing, deep inside, he began to have doubts about those saucers, doubts about his own reason. Perhaps they were not just machines. Never admitting to himself the possibility of contact with other worlds, Mason began to feel that reality might be infinitely greater and more mysterious than he had ever imagined.

Marisa, too, felt better. Listening to Mason singing to himself upstairs, remembering how Carlos ran like a tattered clown through the rubble heaps and how the saucers, whenever they had looked at her, had become *softer*—the glare of their lights fading to a gentle glow, their business-like chatter shifting to a lilting hum, a *lullaby* almost—she smiled to herself in the darkness. She felt better. Safer.

Suddenly one evening she opened her eyes wide. She looked at her plaster saint. She had just realized, to her astonishment, that she hadn't thought about Hector in days.

Frank Riley watched Faye closely. She still drifted un-anchored through other times and places. Sometimes she still talked with people Frank couldn't see. When she spoke about Carlos, she often called him Bobby and went to the front windows of the cafe to look for him, saying, "Frank, that boy's late for supper again. Is he all right? You think he's all right?" But in the days following the saucers' arrival, it seemed to Frank that these lapses became fewer and shorter, that she shared more time with him in the reality of the cafe. Could it really be true? Might she really be getting better? "I dunno. I dunno . . ." Frank murmured to himself.

And yet. . .

When Mike O'Malley returned with the young sergeant, Frank was behind the counter. He chuckled as he watched them climb slowly out of their cruiser, regarding the building as if they were in a dream. They looked at each other, stared, scratched their heads, and finally came inside, setting the little bell tinkling above the door.

"Afternoon, boys," Frank said. "What'll it be?"

"Frank, what the hell's goin' on here?"

"Whatd'ya mean, Mike?"

"Whatd'ya mean, *what do I mean?* Yesterday, we came in here, this place is a disaster area. *Now* look at it!"

The younger cop peered under the tables, took a look behind the counter. "You gotta crew of gremlins in here, Frank? Gnomes? Howd'ya get this done *overnight*?"

"Well, when you're in business, you got to keep up a certain standard, know what I mean? You can't let things get run down. We noticed yesterday the place was looking a bit tatty, Faye and me, so we made a call to . . . to people we know and had it fixed up."

"Yeah," Mike O'Malley said, nodding, sinking slowly into a chair. "It's like it used to be, Frank. Like the old days. Remember I used to come in when I was on the beat?"

Frank nodded.

"It's like something out of a movie," the younger one said. "A real old movie."

They ordered coffee, and Faye brought it. She was humming. She looked radiant. "They sure did a nice job, didn't they? Those little fellas? You shoulda seen them, Mike, flying around here. Course, we couldn't understand a word they were saying, but that doesn't matter among friends, does it?"

"Where, uh, where they from, Faye?"

"Who knows? Way, *way* out. Right now they're on the roof."

Both policemen looked at the ceiling.

"Doing some patching up there, are they?"

Faye shook her head. "They're in the pigeon coop."

Mike O'Malley sipped his coffee, nodding slowly. The younger man rubbed his chin.

"See," Faye went on, "what we hope is that when they trust us a little more, when we understand each other a little better . . ."

"Pigeon coop," Mike said.

Faye nodded.

"Faye, we're old friends, right?"

She nodded again. "You can tell me the truth, huh? You know we're not gonna hassle you, Frank and you."

"Sure, Mike."

Mike jerked his head towards the roof. "You got illegal aliens up there, Faye?"

"What? *Aliens!* Oh no, Mike! Not aliens!"

"We better have a look," the young cop said quietly, into his coffee, but Mike shook his head. He turned to look at his partner as Faye hurried away to wait on two construction workers who had just come in. His eyes were very skeptical and weary, the eyes of a man who had seen it all many times, many, many times, but who in spite of everything had kept a little shining core of kindness deep inside. "Look, Marty," he said. "I've known these folks for twenty years. Longer maybe. They've had ups and downs, but mostly downs. I've never seen them so happy. If they're happy, they're gonna make other folks happy, too. Believe me. So, whoever they got up on that roof, I don't care what size they are, or what color they are, or where they came from, they are not gonna be bothered by *this* cop. Okay?"

The younger man nodded.

"Finished your coffee?"

"Yeah."

"Let's go, then. See you, Frank."

"Take care, Mike."

"Listen, when those guys get finished up on the roof, you send 'em over to my place, okay? I got a '77 Pontiac needs a little work."

Frank laughed and waved, spreading his arms. "All you gotta do is ask," he said.

* * *

The following afternoon, several customers arrived from the construction site. They were tired, and hot, and grimy. They wore hard hats, and some had gloves sticking out of hip pockets. All day, surrounded by the dust and by the clamor of their machines, they had glanced towards the cafe, and when coffee-break time came, they ambled over.

One of them was Gus, the driver of Chief Broom. He was a simple and unimaginative man who took pride in his work and put in an honest day. He worried about his wife's health. He worried about his kid's marks. Sometimes he got a little bitter. Sometimes, a little mean.

He knew how Frank hated him and Chief Broom. Sometimes he liked to go over to the cafe just to get the old guy going. Just for a laugh. "What's *he* doing here?" Frank would shout. "Get him out! No goddam bulldozer drivers allowed in here! Out, out!" Laughing, Gus would stroll back to the site, and one of the other guys would bring him out what he wanted.

That afternoon, however, he got a different reception.

"C'mon in, boys!" Frank called from behind the counter. "Make yourselves at home. Be right with you."

The place looked terrific. It looked like something out of Gus's boyhood. Most of the men sat at tables, but Gus and one of the laborers went to the stools at the counter. "Soda fountain," Gus said, slapping the marble top, staring at the rest of the cafe.

The other man smiled warily. He had not been in New York very long, and his English was not too good. He thought Gus had said something rude.

"*Soda* fountains, you know. When I was a kid, we used to come to places like this and have sodas. Big marble counters, just like this. Shiny tall taps with big handles, just like *those*. And there were these guys behind the counter wearing little white wedge caps, soda-jerks, we called 'em, and they'd scoop ice cream into a tall glass, like *those*—see?—and then pour on the topping of whatever flavor you wanted, and then, and *then*"—Gus's eyes lit up and his hands spread as if he were about to conjure a miracle—"they'd take the glass over to one of those taps, and pull the handle, and squirt a thin stream of fizz in there, like a needle. Fill it up with fizz."

"Pizz?" the other man asked, frowning.

"Fizz. *Fizz!*" Gus made little explosive, foaming sounds.

Frank came to wait on them, rubbing his hands. "What'll it be, boys?"

Gus ordered hamburgers for them both, and strawberry sodas.

And then, something happened that caused the man sitting beside Gus to think about the simpler life that he had left behind in a place where houses were made of mud and straw and where people reclined in hammocks during long evenings, talking softly, and where donkeys could be heard braying in the hills.

He saw a flying saucer.

Frank had placed two hamburger patties on a plate beside the grill and left them for a moment while he went for a fresh package of buns. The saucer flew into the kitchen and hovered over the frozen meat. A dishlike structure on its belly went suddenly red-hot, then white-hot. It executed a shimmying little dance over first one patty and then the other. Then, as silently and unobtrusively as it had come, it drifted back along the counter and out through the door. Behind, the two patties sputtered and steamed on their plate, oozing juices.

"Here ya go, boys," Frank served them up.

"Thanks." Gus slathered on a generous helping of mustard and onions and prepared for the first bite. "You know," he said to the man beside him, "when I was a kid . . ."

But the other man was sliding slowly off his stool, wide eyes fixed on the steaming burger. He looked at Gus, looked back at his plate, pointed to the place above the counter where Pa saucer had hovered. "Youpho!" he said.

"What?"

"Youpho! There!" The man made buzzing sounds and a hovering motion with his hand. "Cook meat!"

"Course it's cooked. Eat it. It's gettin' cold."

"Oh no, senor. I no eat!" He backed up slowly, pushing everything away from him—Gus, the counter, the cooling hamburger, the vanished vision, and Frank, who was staring at him.

He turned and ran.

"Hey, what's wrong with him?"

"Who knows?" Gus munched happily. "Don't worry, I'll pay. I'll eat 'em both. Good burgers. Too bad when this place is gone."

Frank laughed. "Don't hold your breath," he said. "Two sodas?"

"Sure," Gus said. "Why not. Like old times."

Mason Baylor had one more disturbing experience with the saucers, but as Frank told him afterward, he should have known better. "Remember what I said? Mysteries and miracles you should leave alone. Don't pry! Quickest way to end them is to want to know about them!"

For the first time, he had begun to notice the pregnant and lonely girl in apartment 3C, the girl with the wistful smile. What a shame that she should be living all alone, that she should have no one to help her. Without realizing it, Mason Baylor began to think a lot about Marisa Esquivel.

* * *

That morning they met on the steps of 817 East Ninth as she was going out to do her marketing. On impulse he offered to go with her, to carry the bags for her, and to his delight she agreed, smiling. They did the shopping and then had lunch together, laughing often, at ease with one another.

When they returned, he found his door ajar and Pa saucer resting on a footstool inside, plugged into an outlet. He seemed to be asleep. Mason put a finger to his lips. He set down the bag of groceries, tiptoed across the room, and found a magnifying glass amid the clutter on his workbench.

Marisa watched doubtfully. "Mason, Mr. Riley's right. I don't think you should. Honest. Remember what happened last time."

"I just want to have a little *look,*" he whispered. "He's not gonna mind *that,* is he?"

He tiptoed back to the footstool and leaned close, peering through the glass.

What he saw did not disperse the mystery—it deepened it. Looking into the little saucer was like gazing into star-filled heavens on a still night. It was like looking down on a city from far above, or into a dazzling dream-space. And, moving through that space, there were . . . *inhabitants*. Or *something*. Lights streaked down glowing arteries, and clusters of color congregated at intersections and then dispersed again, whizzing off into darkness. Far away, very far away, Mason believed he heard the buzz of . . . conversation?

Mason gaped. He adjusted the glass, beginning to focus more clearly, but as he did so, outraged sounds came from inside Pa. Metallic sounds. Out of a hatch shot a silver arm. On the end was a small but perfect replica of a human hand.

The arm swung.

The hand swatted.

The magnifying glass spun across the room. The arm fell off, the hatch clanged shut, and Pa saucer zoomed away, hissing.

Marisa giggled.

Mason poked at the discarded arm and then picked it up. "For something so small that was some clout!" He squinted, and then retrieved his magnifying glass. "Hey! Look what this says! Sunbeam! My coffeepot! Incredible!"

"The incredible thing," Marisa said, "is you didn't lose your nose."

"But don't you see? They imitate, and they have a sense of humor!"

Harry, meantime, was making the same discovery with Ma saucer. She had drifted in through his open door and was hovering in front of his TV, which, as usual, was on. It was like white noise for Harry, just something that absorbed all distraction—traffic sounds, destruction and construction sounds, domestic sounds drifting down from above. Human sounds.

Harry crept toward the little saucer and smiled.

Ma rotated a little, acknowledging him, and then turned back to the screen. She seemed fascinated by what was happening there. Harry looked.

A beauty pageant was in progress. Leggy women in bathing suits and high heels strutted across the stage to the accompaniment of applause and music.

Ma watched intently, settling down on Harry's rug and propping herself up with a tiny strut that telescoped out from an underside hatch. When the contestants had marched offstage and been replaced by a L'eggs commercial, she suddenly spun up in a little spiral that ended right in front of Harry. She hovered there, turning towards his kitchen table, then back again.

"Something you want over there? Be my guest."

Over she went. In seconds, all of Harry's metal modeling tools vanished—his tiny screwdrivers and pliers, his knife blades and clamps. Leaning close, Harry could hear tiny clipping, pounding, scraping, welding sounds. Then, to his delight, two hatches swung open and out stretched two silvery legs, perfect replicas of the legs of the swim-suited beauty queens, complete with high-heeled shoes.

"Hey!" Harry shouted, clapping. "Go for it!"

Wobbly and unsure, the little saucer started to stroll around the table. By the time she returned to Harry's side, she could execute a little shuffling, swaying dance and take a bow.

Neither of them noticed Pa drifting through the open door. The first sign of his presence was a fierce chattering as he swooped past Harry's ear and landed on the table so hard he skidded, scattering Harry's model kits onto the floor. Out of him shot a silver gripper, which clutched an-grily at the legs of his mate. She danced neatly back and avoided him, uttering a series of merry high-pitched squeals. Again Pa lunged and again she avoided him, this time with a little jump that tucked the legs up against her underside. Airborne, she soared over the opened model box, dropped the legs inside, and swept through the door. Chattering, red lights flashing, Pa zoomed after her.

For a long time Harry sat still, grinning, shaking his head in wonderment. After a while he gathered up the scattered model pieces and arranged them in order on his table. In the box, the leglike appendages gleamed. He took them out carefully, wrapped them in Kleenex, and put them into a corner of his drawer.

Later that night, as they had done every evening since

the arrival of the saucers, the tenants gathered on the roof, which by now, resembled a patio. They brought chairs up from the abandoned apartments. From the storage room in the basement Frank salvaged a table with an umbrella in the center—something left over from an experiment with a sidewalk cafe years before. Mason provided candles, and Marisa donated a few plants. Faye made a large jug of iced tea for them all, and . . .

"Voila!" Frank exclaimed, spreading his arms. "A roof garden!"

Here in the evening, a respectful distance from the pigeon coop, they gathered to relax, to sip their drinks, and to contemplate their visitors. "It's like a castle up here," Mason said, gazing over the parapet at the city and its far-off bustle of sounds. "Like a fantasy. Can't last."

"Oh?" Frank glanced at Faye, who was sitting quietly with her hands folded in her lap, watching the passage of aircraft lights across the sky. "Who says? Some fantasies last forever."

"Oh!" Marisa exclaimed. "Mason, feel!" She took Mason's hand and placed it on her swollen belly.

"Hey! He kicked!"

"You know," Harry said at last, his deep voice rumbling like a distant truck, "I been thinkin'."

They all turned to look at him. Harry did not speak often. Sometimes it seemed that only his huge body was with them, while the rest of him was off in other times and places. "You mean," Frank had said once to Mason, "you mean you don't know who this guy *is?* Harry Noble? You never saw him fight?"

Mason shook his head.

"Well, he was just the best heavyweight in this state! Maybe in this country. Man, you shoulda seen that left! Pow!" And Frank had gone on at length to describe fights of Harry's that he remembered vividly, all those years afterwards. Harry's strength, Harry's speed, Harry's footwork . . . and finally Harry's bad luck.

Harry had sat placidly smiling through all this as if he were deaf, watching lights in the sky that no one else could see.

So, on that evening when he said, "I been thinkin'," and leaned forward with his elbows on his knees and his massive palms outstretched, they all paid attention. Even Faye looked at him.

"What we got here," Harry said, looking at the quiet pigeon coop and then at his left hand, "is one male"—he looked at his right hand—"and one female."

His audience leaned closer, waiting.

"I been thinkin' . . ." Harry brought his hands together.

There was a long silence.

Faye was the first to understand. "Babies!"

Marisa's eyes went wide.

Mason sprawled back in his chair as if kayoed by the suggestion. "Wait a minute, wait a minute," he said, waving his hands. "We don't know what they are or where they come from, but we do know that they're machines, right? *Machines*." He looked from one face to the other. "Machines don't . . ."

"I'm not so *sure* about that," Faye said sternly. "Just because you don't understand, Mason . . ."

"No. No. Wait a minute!"

"You know, Mason," Frank said, "when you think about it, Harry might have something. Look."

"At what?"

"That. Look at that pile of metal. Pots, appliances, wire, nuts and bolts, you name it."

Harry nodded slowly.

"Repairs," Mason said. "Self-maintenance."

"Some of it, sure, but not *that* much. Why, there's enough there to make four or five . . ."

"Something else," Harry said. Again they all waited through the long pause before he finished. "He's jealous."

"Pa?" Mason laughed. "Jealous?"

Harry nodded.

Faye slapped Mason's arm. "See? They got emotions. You can't tell me any *machine's* got emotions."

"I still can't believe . . ."

At that moment the saucers returned. They came home in perfect formation from the northwest, joined together like a single creature. They came so fast they seemed to materialize. Their first pass took them right across the roof and out over the vacant lots, so fast that all the humans heard was a sound like soft silk tearing. They climbed, slowed, banked, and returned in a looping dive that took them around the roof garden and straight into the pigeon coop.

Immediately, the familiar eerie radiance began. This time, however, it was brighter than anything so far. It was as if a huge, shimmering searchlight, hidden under that metallic trash heap, were being turned on, gradually brightening to full intensity. Dazzled, blinking, the humans watched as the junk pile was transformed by this brilliance into something beautiful, a shimmering, silvery mass like a galaxy far away in the clear night. It lit up the whole roof-top, the whole neighborhood. It was so bright that it lit the walls of distant buildings and brought startled people to their windows. It was so bright that the little group on the roof, their eyes firmly closed now, believed that they could actually *feel* the radiance like a life-giving current trembling in every pore and molecule.

No one thought. They felt. They knew.

Smiling throughout it all, Marisa spread her hands on the infant in her womb.

"Far . . . out!" Mason said when the light faded and the trembling died down. "Super . . . natural!"

Ecstatic, Faye clasped her hands. "It must be the Fourth of July! It must be *ten* Fourths of July!"

Frank sat, gaping.

Harry nodded solemnly. He leaned forward. "I been thinkin' . . ."

They all turned to him.

"I been thinkin' that it would be neighborly to bring what they need most. What they're gonna need a lot of. Bring it right up here where they can get it easy."

"What's that?" Marisa asked.

"Electricity," Harry said.

And so they did. Out of closets and storage rooms, out of Harry's workshop and the old janitor's room beside the furnace, they gathered extension cords and strung them together from the highest working outlet in the building, along the fourth-floor corridor, up the last flight of stairs, and out onto the roof. Even then there was not quite enough cord to bring the last plug close to the coop.

"Wait," Frank said. "I got an idea." Minutes later he returned with a long chain of Christmas lights. "Got them for the outdoor cafe years ago," he said. "Used to be real nice down there."

"Looks to me as if it's gonna be real nice up here," Mason said, as they strung the lights from strut to strut around their roof garden and secured the plug on a steel support beam near the coop. *"We'll* enjoy it, anyway."

"Okay." He called down the stairs to Marisa, who called the message along to Harry.

"Plug it in!"

So the neighbors in other buildings were now treated to

another astonishing sight. Cupping their hands to their windows, they saw a building they had thought doomed to darkness, now adorned with a festive circle of light, like a triumphant crown.

"He gets so *dirty!*" Faye said later in her bedroom as Marisa turned the pages of her album, looking at pictures of Bobby. "He'd tinker under that Ford all night if I'd let him. Sometimes I have to haul him out by the sneakers. Heaven knows, that car's the most important thing in the world to him." She rummaged in a closet and found an old T-shirt, caked with grease. "Look at that! That's gonna take some special detergent, isn't it? That's the kind of thing you see on the *before* half of the commercials." She laughed. "Lots more here. Look, I've even got his baby pajamas, and his first shoes, see? Probably I've even got some diapers in here somewhere. Can't throw anything away..." Her voice drifted off.

Turning the pages of the album, the chronicle of Bobby's life, Marisa came at last to a photograph of a handsome, smiling youth of perhaps eighteen. It was obviously a graduation photograph, but turning brown at the edges, and the young man's hair was close-cropped—a crewcut. Peeking out from underneath was a yellowing newspaper clipping, folded tight and small. Marisa did not take it out to read it. After this page there was nothing. The rest of the album was empty. Blank.

"Mrs. Riley..."

"Some nights, like tonight, Bobby doesn't come home till real late, and Frank gets worried, you know. Kids, he says. Kids and cars..."

"Mrs. Riley, how old is Bobby?"

"How old? Why, let's see...He's just had a birthday. Just...only last..." She leaned over and squinted at the picture, wraithlike, lost in another time. "He has his father's ears, hasn't he? Too bad he and Frank don't get along better, but it's often the way with young men, isn't it? When they get older, they get more tolerant, sometimes. More understanding . . ." Again her voice drifted off. Her head sank like a child's on Marisa's shoulder.

Marisa folded up the scrapbook. "It's a lovely album," she said. "It's really beautiful, Mrs. Riley." She set the book on Faye's bedside table and stood up slowly, gently lowering Faye to her pillows as she did so. The old lady was so frail, her hair so white, the crisscrossing lines on her face so sad! "In we go," Marisa said, drawing up the covers and tucking her in. "Sleep well, Mrs. Riley."

"Call me Faye, dear."

"All right. Faye."

Faye smiled drowsily. "You are such a beautiful child."

Marisa turned out the light.

"And you are going to enjoy being a mother so much. It's so . . . wonderful . . ."

Softly, Marisa closed the door.

8

RIGHT AWAY CARLOS knew he should not have done it.

He should not have told the others about being zapped by flying saucers. More than anything, even more than crawling into that coop in the first place, Carlos regretted telling Ramirez, and Al, and Poncho.

They thought he was playing some strange joke.

"Saucers," Ramirez said.

"Whoosh, whoosh?" Poncho asked, making little swooping gestures with both hands.

"Like, outer space?" Al asked. "Like *Star Wars?* Like beam me up?"

"Yeah! Only *little!*" Eyes wide, Carlos gestured the approximate size of the creature he had glimpsed in the second before being almost electrocuted. "With *big eyes!*"

"Yeah?" Ramirez nodded solemnly. "How many?"

Al smirked, scuffed at a piece of refuse with his heel. "Carlos, what were you *on*, man?"

"Nothin'! I tell ya . . ."

"Yeah," Poncho said. "Tell us again, Carlos. Start with when the trash can grabbed your bat and flew away. That's the really good part. I really like that part."

"Naw," Ramirez said. "The best part is where the saucepan attacks him."

"Part I like best," Al said, "is where Carlos crawls into the . . . what was it again?"

"Pigeon coop!" Carlos said, glaring.

"Gotta watch those electric pigeons," Ramirez said.

"Look, just forget it, okay? Just forget I ever told you about it."

They all shrugged. "Sure, Carlos. Sure."

"Hey, Al," Poncho said. "I ever tell you about the fish comin' outta the tap at our place?"

"No!"

"Yeah! Fish, all colors. There was purple fish, pink fish, blue fish . . ."

It was a bad time for Carlos. The episode itself had undermined his confidence. And now, because in a weak moment he had told about it, it threatened to strip him of his dignity.

What next?

Carlos had taken Lacey's money to get those people out of that building, and somehow he had to do it. If he failed, he might as well move to another part of town, because there would be no more contracts coming down in Lacey's neighborhoods, not for him.

He would never admit it, but he was frightened.

"Boop, boop," said Al. "Pac-Men from Mars. Boop, boop."

"Very funny."

They were all climbing the stairs of a gutted building across the construction site from 817 East Ninth.

"Boop, boop, boop. Spock to Carlos. Spock to Carlos . . ." Al used two paper plates to make an unearthly flapping mouth, and Ramirez and Poncho broke up with laughter.

"You guys," Carlos swung around, pointing. "You got no sensitivity. No gratitude. That's what's the matter with you."

"Boop boop. Boop boop de boop!"

Carlos grabbed Al by the shirt front and slammed him against the old wall, cracking plaster and lath. His stomach clenched into hard little knots. "Enough!"

"Okay! Okay!" Al held his hands up. "It was just a joke, for godsake!"

"I don't need your jokes! So shut up! You hear me?"

They reached the roof. The three others clustered into a surly little group while Carlos pulled a pair of Army binoculars out of his shirt and focused them on the roof of 817. There was the pigeon coop, there was the crown of lights that he had seen blazing the night before, and there, looking back at him through her own pair of ancient binoculars, was Faye.

She waved.

Carlos dropped his glasses.

Behind him, the others snickered.

Carlos whirled around. "Those people, you know what they got? They got solidarity! They got somethin' helpin' them that *we* ain't got! They're *organized!*"

The Crusaders shrugged. Poncho and Al sprawled amidst the rubble of the roof. Ramirez cranked up the volume on his tape machine and went into a little shuffle, wide-eyed.

Carlos squatted down and slid his binoculars up over the parapet.

"Hey, Carlos," Al called. "You afraid that old lady's

gonna *look* at you? You afraid she's gonna send little space machines, zip-zip, over to slice you up? That what you afraid of?"

Carlos snarled an obscenity and peered through the glasses. Mrs. Riley was sitting at the table with Marisa and Mason. They were laughing together and drinking something that she was pouring out of an icy pitcher into tall glasses.

"Lemonade!" Carlos said under his breath. He had not drunk lemonade since he was a very small boy. His father, whom he could not remember too clearly, had taken him to a cafe like Rileys'. They had drunk lemonade out of tall, sweating glasses. For an instant, the sweet-sour taste of the liquid drifted across his tongue. Ice cubes chilled his lip. He swallowed.

"Bobby's over there," Faye said.

"Where?" Mason got up and looked.

"Over there on the roof of that old building. Don't pay any attention. He's playing some game with binoculars. He and some friends. He wants to pretend that we don't see him. What a boy!" She laughed gently and sipped her lemonade.

Mason and Marisa glanced at each other.

Inside the pigeon coop, there were tiny bangs and clangs and hisses. Lights flickered as if miniature welding torches were busily at work.

Faye got up to have a closer look.

Marisa ate fruit. "You want some papaya? It's good. I can't stop eating it."

"No, thanks," Mason said. He looked at her swelling tummy. "When's the baby due?"

"I'm not sure."

"How can you not be sure. I thought those things were fairly predictable."

"Yes, but, well, I haven't been to a doctor."

"What? That's crazy!"

"I know. I should go, but I feel fine."

"But you have to take care of yourself! Take care of *both* of you! You gotta have proper food—vitamins, and milk, and celery! Celery's *very* good, I think."

Marisa took a large bite of papaya. "I know what's good. I just know. I feel it here." She grinned and rubbed her belly. "Besides, my boyfriend's coming soon, and he'll look after me."

"Your boyfriend?"

"Um-hum. Hector. He's a musician, so he moves around a lot. That's why you haven't seen him. Here and there, different places. He moves around. But he's coming back soon, and then he'll stay and look after us."

"Where is he now?"

She shrugged.

"He doesn't write?"

"Uh-unh."

"Or call?"

"No. That's not like Hector. He'll just show up one day."

"But . . . but isn't he *worried* about you? If I . . ."

"Oh, *sure,* he's worried. He sent money in January."

"Nothing since *January?"*

"Well, things are hard, being an artist. *You* know, I guess."

Mason nodded. "Look, Marisa. You know what you should do? You should take that cash from Lacey and move out. Go to a better place. Better for the baby."

For a moment Marisa was silent, and then slowly, she shook her head.

"Why not?"

"Well, for one thing, Hector might have trouble finding me when he comes back. For another thing"—she turned to look at Mason—"we've started to make things better right here, haven't we? And do you know what I think? I think we can keep right on doing that!"

There was a burst of enthusiastic clattering from inside the coop. Leaning close, Faye laughed and clapped. She picked up a few nuts and bolts lying nearby on the roof and tossed them inside.

Mason nodded towards the coop and the saucers. "What do you think they *are?*"

"I told you. I don't think we ought to ask."

"But it doesn't make sense."

Marisa laughed. "Lots of things in life don't make sense. You hadn't noticed? No sense at all."

"But *flying saucers?*"

"Who knows? Maybe that's not what they *really* are. Maybe that's just the way we have to see them. A kind of *disguise,* you know? What they think we might understand, might not be too afraid of."

"You mean *forces?*"

"Maybe. But we shouldn't ask. We should leave it mysterious. Why are you *smiling,* Mason?"

"Because it's so incredible! Because I know. . ."

"You *know.* What do you know?"

"Well, I know something about *physics,* for one thing. And something about space travel for another. There are laws, you know. Physical laws. I don't believe . . ."

Marisa plunked down her glass of lemonade and stood up abruptly. "That's the trouble, right there! You don't *believe!* You invent a few little laws, you shoot up a few rockets, and you think you know everything about time and the universe!"

"Whoa! Wait a minute! Hold on!"

"You get so obsessed that you don't *see* any other reality. Not even when it's right in front of you. Not even when it's a miracle. There isn't room for what's mysterious anymore. And do you know what happens when mystery dies? Your *soul* dies, too! All you'll have left then is mathematics, and whatever you can *measure!*"

Head high, one hand holding her belly, Marisa turned and strode towards the stairs. She took the first step down and then turned back, gripping the banister. "And I thought you were an *artist*," she said.

By the time Marisa got to her apartment, she was hot, and tired, and crying. Her feet hurt. The baby seemed pounds heavier. She brushed tears away as she closed the door and locked it, sliding the bolt and clipping the chain in place. She sank into her armchair and stared a long time at the window, at the gauze drapes billowing like sails in the breeze. They made her think of long and carefree journeys, and for a little while she dreamed, letting tears roll down her face until they dried.

Only after she had blown her nose and gone to the kitchen for a glass of orange juice, did she look at the pictures in her apartment.

She had not gotten used to having them. She had not even hung them up. They leaned against walls and furniture.

When she saw them, she felt better.

For one thing, they were all paintings of 817 East Ninth and the neighborhood that she knew. She could recognize corners, storefronts, even hydrants from which firemen would sometimes let the water spray for happy kids. Yet, there was something else that Marisa loved. They were full of vitality and vigor. They were so luminous with life that every building seemed lit with magical light *inside*. Sometimes in the afterglow on summer evenings, Marisa had seen such a light—a light that brought things alive in ways beyond human imagination.

The painter of those canvases, Marisa believed, was a genius.

The paintings were Mason's.

All of them.

They were the ones he had hurled through his window in a beery fit the night Pamela left, on that night when Carlos had come, smashing her statue and throwing money. Marisa had sat in the darkness in her apartment, listening. She heard clumps and bangs. She heard cans rolling across the floor. And finally she had heard that crash on her windowsill and had looked up to see the painting of the old neighborhood balancing there before it toppled backward to the street. Then she had watched in horror as Mason's other paintings spun away into the night like so many pieces of garbage.

Without knowing exactly why, without even thinking about it, Marisa had hurried out to save them. She had counted fifteen as they sailed away into the darkness, and she tried to see where they fell. One by one she found them, all ripped, their frames shattered, and hauled them upstairs to her flat. It took a lot of work. By the time she found the thirteenth she was exhausted, and it was almost 3 a.m. The last she had discovered deep in the Lacey Plaza excavation, one under a trailer, and the other wedged into the treads of a bulldozer. By 3:30 she had them all in her apartment. She had saved them; at least, she had saved what was left of them, but when she looked at them she felt sick. That was the way she had gone to bed, feeling sick and exhausted.

Next morning, the paintings were fixed.

At first she had been so awed by her restored status that

she hadn't noticed that the paintings had been touched by the same magic; but when she turned around, there they were, all of them, glowing like new.

Things had happened so fast after that she hadn't had a chance to tell Mason what she had done, and what the saucers had done. She wasn't sure whether he'd be pleased or not, because she didn't know him, really. But, curled in her armchair, sipping her orange juice while she gazed at those luminous paintings, she knew that he was inspired and infuriating.

Through his binoculars, Carlos checked out 817 East Ninth from the top down. He watched the brief argument between Mason and Marisa. He watched Marisa leave. He saw Harry sitting on the front steps, polishing old trophies. He saw Frank, wearing his apron, emerge from the door of the cafe and stretch in the sunlight. He saw him joke with some departing customers and wave to them as they crossed the street on their way back to work. Focusing the glasses, Carlos saw that Frank was smiling! Laughing!

Incredible! These people ought to be frightened down to their toes. They ought to be packing as fast as they could. They ought to be moving out. And yet, here they were, perfectly calm, perfectly . . . *confident*. They looked *safe* inside that little world, as if they had some clout, some *leverage*.

"Hey, *boss*," Poncho said, and Carlos did not miss the sarcasm in the way he spoke that word, "we gonna sit here and get a suntan, or we gonna do a job?"

"Those people," Al said. "Looks to me like they ain't got the message yet."

Eyes slits, dancing in little circles, Ramirez cranked up the volume of his tape machine until it became a pounding, insulting noise.

"Turn it down!" Carlos ordered, but no one could hear him anymore. No one was interested in hearing him anymore.

Carlos spun around, strode across the roof, and knocked the recorder spinning off Ramirez's shoulder. It crashed, squawked, went silent.

"You're gonna *pay,* man! You gonna pay for that machine!"

"Am I, Ramirez? *Am* I? *Am* I?" Carlos kept crowding in tight, keeping the other man off balance and staggering, until Ramirez was backed up hard against the chimney, with Carlos's forearm across his throat and Carlos's fist poised level with his belly. "When I tell you somethin', *you do it!"* Carlos spoke softly, but the arm pressed hard, twisting the man's head and forcing his jaw up.

Ramirez sneered. "Not anymore, man. Take a look."

Carlos looked. Poncho was there behind him. And Al. They were standing with their feet apart, braced, hefting cudgels they had grabbed from the debris on the roof. Like Ramirez, they were smiling.

Al lifted his chin. "Unless you wanna get hurt, Carlos ol' buddy, back off! Go check out some U...F...Os!"

Poncho said nothing. He showed his teeth. He showed rusty nails in the end of his club.

Carlos backed off.

"Now then," Ramirez said, rubbing his throat and neck. "You are goin' in one direction, Carlos my friend, and the Crusaders are goin' in another. And why? Because you have lost your *nerve,* is why! You are *gutless!* You are *bad...luck!* You are *history!"*

"You punks," Carlos said. "Without me you'll be shakin' down parking meters. Grabbin' handbags!"

Ramirez smiled. "We are gonna part friends, and the

way that we're gonna do that is you will pay our cuts from the Lacey job. Now." He held out his hand.

Carlos shrugged. "Why not? It's yours." He pulled out his wallet and counted six $100 bills.

Ramirez transferred these to his left hand and held out his right again. "Plus three hundred. For the machine."

Carlos counted out more bills.

Ramirez patted him on the cheek. "Adios, amigo. You were a good man once."

"Yeah," Al said, "before you started seein' things."

"Before you lost your *cojones*," Poncho said, grinning, backing up with the others towards the rickety stairs. "Before you got scared of pregnant broads and old women."

"Go to hell!" Carlos said, waving his arm. "You slow me down anyway."

But for a long time after they had gone, after their laughter faded in the stairwell like sand draining out of the broken building, Carlos stood where they had left him, his face working, his hands plunged deep in his pockets. He had never felt more alone, or more helpless, or more frightened. He felt like a kid again, being led to the agency, wondering where his mother was.

He turned towards the building he had been hired to clear. There it was, standing proudly on the far side of the Lacey Plaza site. A hard hat was coming out of Rileys' Cafe with a tray loaded with styrofoam coffee cups. Harry Noble, finished with his trophy polishing, was now sweeping the steps of the apartment entrance. Carlos lifted his glasses and looked. Incredible! Harry was dancing! He was doing a perfect soft-shoe, in time to the beat of his broom.

Carlos swung the glasses up, up, past the four storys of windows staring like empty eyes, to the roof. There, serenely gazing back at him through her own binoculars, was Faye.

She waved.

Before he realized what he was doing, Carlos waved back.

9

WHEN MASON BAYLOR wanted to think, he walked. That night he walked fifteen blocks, and just before eleven o'clock he was returning along Avenue C to East Ninth. He was thinking about Marisa—her indignation when she had said to him, "Do you think you can *know* everything?" And her eyes, so disappointed, as if she had expected much more from him.

That question had hurt. He was an artist, and he understood that knowledge was more than facts, more than anything expressible in language, or in any mathematical system. He knew that most reality must lie beyond human understanding. He understood what Marisa was saying: that whatever entered human experience from the world beyond must appear in a form that humans could comprehend. To appear at all, in other words, it must become mechanical. It must imitate, and the very imitation would be a sign of yearning to make contact, despite the worlds of difference.

They *were* a force, these saucers. And what need did a force have of toasters, and frying pans, and nuts and bolts, except to refurbish itself in a way that humans could comprehend? What need did it have of the difference between sexes, except to show humans that it understood them? And what need did it have to repair a decrepit building, except to make an overture?

"Of course!" Mason said, laughing suddenly, slamming his fist into his left palm.

And what other shape could this force take? Humanoid? Absurd! Animal? Vegetable? Confusing, and undignified, too! Ghostly? Too insubstantial! No, the saucer was the *only* shape, the perfect shape to suggest the effortless sliding between layers of time and space.

So. Here they were. Rotund handy-persons. Prickly little fixers. And soon, if Harry's hunch was right . . .

Mason rounded the last corner. Eight-seventeen East Ninth stood among the ruins, half a block ahead. No lights shone in the apartment windows, but he could see light spilling out of Rileys' Cafe. Light spilled also through the window of the Rileys' second-floor apartment, and from Marisa's window above.

Suddenly all the lights in the building, even the ones that had been dark one second before, blazed fiercely and began to flash.

The glare was so intense that Mason staggered back, shielding his eyes. "Marisa!" he shouted. He ran.

The time was exactly 11:03.

No one saw what happened in the coop at 11:03 that night. Everyone was somewhere else. Mason was returning from his walk. Marisa was helping Faye get ready for bed.

Harry and Frank were cleaning up the cafe.

Suddenly, all the lights in the building dimmed, brightened, and dimmed again, as if some very thirsty creature had taken a huge gulp of electricity.

"Wha . . ." Frank said.

Harry had already dropped his broom and raced down the hallway, and now he was taking the stairs two at a time. The lights strobed again, and as Mason reached the vestibule, he saw Frank with his apron flapping, racing down the hall in the weird light like some fugitive from a rock-horror video, and he heard Faye screaming above, "This is *it!* This is *IT!*"

"What?" Mason shouted. *"Where's Marisa?"*

No one answered. They were all headed for the roof. He ran after them.

The strobing quickened as he climbed, and then faded to a long stretch of dimness. Something was sucking up all the electricity in the building. Mason thought he could hear the hum of racing current. He was sure he smelled acrid smoke from burning insulation. He kept running, not even realizing that he had been calling Marisa's name until she called back, "Up here! Hurry!"

The scene on the roof was weird. The Christmas lights had faded to a dim glow, and wisps of smoke rose from the cord. Eerie luminescence shone out of the nest of metal in the pigeon coop, silhouetting Frank and Harry, Faye and Marisa, all of whom were cautiously drawing close to it. This was not the dazzling white blaze that Mason had seen before, but a softer and warmer radiance, vibrating and shimmering like northern lights. Standing near Marisa, peering into the coop, Mason saw that the light came from Ma. She was glowing all over. But she was also humming anxiously, and Mason saw the reason for her concern. The plug that linked her to the power supply had begun to melt.

Pa fluttered around her, uttering plaintive little cries. Twice he hovered close to the humans, closer than he had ever come before.

Suddenly, the building went dark.

"Fuses!" Frank shouted. "She blew the fuses!"

Ma saucer's glow began to fade rapidly. Her cries grew weaker.

"Do something!" Marisa shouted. *"Do* something!"

Frank, Harry and Mason were already running back to the stairs. On their way past, Frank detoured into the cafe for his flashlight, and a few moments later the three of them crowded together in front of the old fuse box in the furnace room. Mason touched it and snapped his hand away. The wires and all the connections were red-hot. Even the meter glowed.

Frank used the corner of his apron to open the door and twist out the blown fuses. "More over there!" he said. "In the cupboard!"

"Not good enough," Harry said, and reaching between them he jammed a rusty garden trowel into the rear of the box, welding the circuit terminals together. Instantly the meter began to purr, then to hum, then to whine. The trowel turned red. Its plastic handle bubbled and drooled away in a sticky mess.

Mason cursed softly. "Harry, you're gonna burn the place down!"

Harry shook his head.

"But *look* at it! Look at the wires!"

Harry gazed calmly at the smoldering insulation, and then at Mason. "You gotta have a little faith," he said. "We take care of them, they take care of us."

Upon on the roof, lights flickered.

"Thank goodness!" Marisa said.

But something had changed during those moments of

darkness. Something extraordinary had happened, unwitnessed by any human eyes. Pa saucer had ceased his agitated hovering, and Ma was no longer whimpering anxiously.

She was purring now.

She glowed.

Beside her were two very small, very new arrivals. They were tiny visitors. They had the same cowled tops as Ma and Pa, the same luminous and protruding orbs, the same projecting stabilizers and antennae. One was more streamlined; the other, bulkier.

There was no question that they were alien. And yet, there was also something . . . something . . .

"Human," Faye said, nodding. "There's something *human* about them."

She was right. For one thing, the rounder saucer was cross-eyed. For another, the more rotund one had in the lower half of his face a curved open space that looked exactly like a mouth. In fact, set at regular intervals into his lower jaw were studs like rudimentary teeth. Most remarkable, however, was the fact that both new arrivals were equipped with legs and articulated feet. The legs of the rounder one were longer and the feet slimmer and more graceful. The little squat fellow with the wide grin sported lumpish, functional, hooflike appendages.

They were, in saucer terms, the equivalents of human babies.

"What a compliment!" Marisa said.

Faye nodded, smiling radiantly.

"Incredible!" Mason whispered, coming up behind them.

"Jeesh!" Frank said.

Harry included everyone, saucers, humans, and heaven, with the single gesture of a huge hand. "Friends," he said, smiling broadly. "All is well!"

But all was not well.

Ma began to behave erratically again. Her light changed from a healthy rose to a bilious yellow. She shuddered. A small grinding emerged from her, as if someone had dropped a spoon into a garbage disposal. Then, clumsily, she shifted to one side, leaving behind a third small saucer.

This one, however, was not like the other two. The others were symmetrical, but this one was misshapen, crunched on one side. The others were furnished with stolid little legs, but this one's legs were rickety and bent. The others' headlights shone mischievously, but no light at all came from the orbs of this newest and tiniest arrival.

The little creature lay still, silent, pathetic.

Whining, Pa zipped over to it, extended electrical terminals, and administered several sharp jolts. Nothing happened. Desperate now, Pa swerved around so that his plug could reach the half-melted socket of the extension cord, made the connection, and tried again. This time the force of the shock sent the lifeless little body spinning into the air, but when it crashed down again (except for the spasmodic twitching of one leg) it was still inert, its eyes dark. A defective hatch fell open. Forlorn parts tumbled onto the roof.

Faye and Marisa wept.

Harry nodded solemnly. "Batteries not included," he said.

"Poor little guy," Frank said.

Mason was moved too, but he was also curious. "Well," he said, "you know, it's only a . . ." *Machine,* he was going to say, but he looked down into four sets of reproachful saucer eyes, and fell silent. He turned his back on them. "Look," he whispered to the other humans. "Whatever you think, this is the perfect chance to, well, you know, see what makes them tick."

"No way," Faye said.

"If it makes you feel better, call it a postmortem. In the interests of science. How can we understand if we don't . . ."

She shook her head firmly.

"She's right," Frank said. "Faye's right, Mason. There are some things we just shouldn't know about."

"You just have to accept," Faye said. Her lip was trembling, and fresh tears brimmed in her eyes.

Frank put his arm around her.

"Isn't that what you said to me, Papa? You just have to accept?"

Frank nodded. He embraced her, and she laid her white head on his shoulder.

"Don't question," she said. "There are some things you'll never understand, never know the reason for." She began to hum softly, a hymn out of another time and place.

"You . . . you think we should *bury* it?" Mason asked, incredulously.

Marisa dried her eyes. "We won't have to do anything," she said. "Do you think they can't look after things? Do you think we can understand what's happening here? Uh-unh. Best thing we can do right now is go away and leave them alone." She took Mason's hand, and they followed Frank and Faye under the lights of the roof garden to the stairs. "You coming, Harry?"

The big man waved and nodded. He'd be right along, he said. But for a long time after the others had gone, Harry Noble stayed. He said nothing. He did nothing. He simply stood and looked with wide and sympathetic eyes at the little group of saucers. They looked back at him.

He waited.

Whatever happened next happened out of time as Harry understood it. It happened not on the roof of an old building in New York City, but in some other region with no clocks, no schedules, no merely human urgencies. It happened wherever feelings were more important than language, or intelligence, or bodies. So, Harry could not have said exactly *when* it happened; but sometime near dawn, just before sunrise, he found himself sitting cross-legged inside the pigeon coop while Pa nudged into his outstretched hands what seemed to be just a small, deformed, defunct piece of machinery. Harry's hands were large enough to enclose it completely. Cradling it, he crossed the roof as the sun rose, and trudged downstairs through the core of the old building, down to his apartment in the basement.

It was a terrible night for Frank. He knew it would be. Faye had been inconsolable. For hours, alternately weeping and laughing, she had wandered through the apartment wearing a black hat, looking for something. She parted the curtains and peered out through all the windows. She carried her scrapbooks into Bobby's bedroom. She even wandered down the hall towards the stairs before Frank woke out of his light sleep, chased after her, and brought her back. At last he gave her warm milk and a sedative, and she settled down then, although she tossed and turned in her sleep, talking to the people in her dreams.

So, when he got up next morning, Frank felt very old and weary, as if all the cushioning had gone out of him and the bones in all his joints were rubbing together. He checked on Faye, found her asleep. He pulled on his clothes and immediately went upstairs to the pigeon coop on the roof.

The saucers had gone.

All of them.

Gone.

The signs of what had happened the night before were still there—the partially melted extension cords, and the scattered pile of metal debris, and the scorched place in the asphalt of the roof. But the saucers themselves had vanished.

Frank nodded bitterly. "I knew it," he said. "Too good to be true." He kicked the end of the extension cord and went back downstairs. He knew what would happen now. Carlos would be coming back—Carlos or someone else. Someone worse. The gangs would gather round for the final assault on the old building and its residents. The street gangs. The business gangs. It was, Frank Riley knew, only a matter of time . . .

He tied on his apron. He went downstairs to open his shop for business.

But the cafe was already open.

The hall door stood ajar. Sunlight poured through from the front windows and flooded the hall. As Frank approached, he heard the jukebox playing Glenn Miller's "String o' Pearls." The music, as beautiful as it had been when he and Faye were young, washed into the hall with the blazing sunlight of the new day. He smelled coffee. He smelled bacon sizzling on the grill. "Wha . . ." he said. "Who . . ."

He stepped through the doorway and saw them.

All four of them.

Pa was cooking the bacon. Ma was raising the blind on the door and turning the sign to OPEN. The two small ones, airborne with tiny legs pumping, were swaying to the music.

"Hey!" Frank said, and when they heard him all four of them formed into a bowing little chorus line of welcome. On the end, the chunkier of the two youngsters broke into an impromptu jive routine. Ma swatted him on the rear end.

Frank Riley clapped his hands, laughing. "We are in *business!*"

And they were.

That day was the liveliest since the fifties. In fact, Frank thought when it was all over that he had *never* been busier. Many new customers arrived—construction workers on their breaks, and mothers bringing kids from blocks away, and people who just happened by. Miraculously, Faye came down to work at seven o'clock as she used to years before, a poised and peppery waitress. "Pan-san," she hollered through the service window. "Scrambled wet, with Canadian on the side! Adam and Eve on a raft! And two over-easy, English, no toast, and hold the spuds."

At the grill, Frank was a genuine short-order cook again. He scowled; he growled; he cursed. He was deliriously happy. It had been many, many years since he had been so utterly swept up in his work, with no time to think and brood. The jukebox played; the cash register kept jingling and ringing; but it was not those sounds that stimulated him so much as the clatter of plates coming and going, and the laughter of friends, and all the wonderful *talk,* the talk going on and on like a big, fresh river.

In the kitchen, unseen by the customers, the saucers flourished.

Pa helped cook. He hovered over the grill, wielding spatula and salt shaker, and he learned fast, after a few early problems. Gus, the bulldozer driver, got a reversed hamburger—two patties enclosing a slice of bun. Gus contemplated it silently before he called Faye over. He pointed.

"Uh-oh," she said, laughing. "Sorry! He's new. Doesn't know what a hamburger is yet."

"Lady, how can you not know what a hamburger is?"

"I'll fix it. No problem. Just take a sec." She shoved the plate back through the service window. *"Show him a picture,"* she muttered to Frank, and Frank did that, rummaging in a drawer for an old advertisement and holding it up in front of his hovering assistant.

"Buns outside!" he shouted. "Got that?"

A minute later, a perfect hamburger materialized for Gus.

Ma looked after desserts. She too worked from pictures, and she learned fast. Of course, at first there was some confusion. She cut gigantic pieces of pie, diced a whole pineapple into one-inch cubes, chopped up a banana with its skin still on.

As for the littlest saucers, they swooped and cavorted, and messed up everything. They loved liquids. The rounder one dove off a shelf into a cauldron of soup, circling happily, a tiny periscope just breaking the surface. The squarish one narrowly escaped being blended into a milkshake; Faye spotted him peering out just as she was about to switch on the machine, his eyes weirdly distorted by the thick glass. "You know what you guys are?" she said, spooning him out. "Flotsam and jetsam, that's what. Little floating bits of stuff." She laughed and pointed to them. "You're Flotsam," she said to the round one, "and *you're* Jetsam!"

When they took a break during a morning lull, she told Frank what she had named them. "Wait till Bobby sees them!" she said.

Frank sighed. "Faye, Bobby. . ."

But then suddenly they were all busy again with a fresh wave of customers, and whatever Frank intended to say was forgotten.

* * *

On the roof of the burnt-out building across the construction site, Carlos did not feel well. His hands trembled, and he had to steady the binoculars against the top of the parapet. He was cold and tired. He had stayed on the roof all night. For most of that time he had simply stared at 817 East Ninth, the building that now obsessed him. At 11:03 he had witnessed the awesome display of lights. It had frightened him, and he had cringed down behind the parapet, mumbling a half-forgotten prayer. Later, he had watched the lights blink out one by one, leaving only that circlet on the roof, that strange crown.

At dawn, he had awakened from a doze to see movement up there, and he focused his glasses on Harry Noble passing solemnly across the roof towards the stairs, his hands extended as if he were going to give or receive an offering.

By then, Carlos was shaking, partly from the chill, partly from hunger and fatigue, partly from fear, but mostly from the awful, helpless feeling of just not knowing what to do.

And so, he was enormously relieved by the sight of Kovacs's limousine pulling up to the cafe just before noon.

Shouting Kovacs's name even before he got to the bottom of the rickety stairs, Carlos ran through the construction site, shirt flying, binoculars bouncing.

Kovacs stared hard at Carlos as he came running up with his arms outstretched, panting.

"Mr. Kovacs! Good to see you, man!"

"Don't touch me, Carlos! You're a mess!"

"Mr. Kovacs, I gotta talk to you."

"No. You have it the wrong way around. I have to talk to *you!*"

"I can explain this . . ."

"Listen, Carlos. Listen."

"What it is . . ."

"Listen to me, Carlos!" Kovacs pointed a warning finger. "You took Mr. Lacey's money, correct?"

"Yes, but . . ."

"A *lot* of money. A good contract. And all you had to do was make sure those people moved out. Voluntarily."

"Yes, but . . ."

"And when was that to have been done, Carlos?"

"Last Monday."

"Last Monday. Right. So tell me, why is it that those people are still there? And why is it that they have actually *improved this building?"*

"Mr. Kovacs . . ."

"Don't *touch* me!"

"Sir, you wouldn't believe me . . ."

"Try me."

"You wouldn't believe me if I just *told* you, know what I mean? I mean, it's the truth, there's a real good reason for all this, but it's so *strange,* it's so *weird,* I can't just *tell* you, I gotta show you. Okay?"

Kovacs looked at his watch.

"Please, Mr. Kovacs. You gotta *see* this."

"How long will it take?"

"Not long. Five minutes, maybe. It's right up there, right up on the roof."

"You want me to climb up there?"

"It's not bad. Honest. Only four flights. We can rest on the way. We can go slow. But I swear to you, Mr. Kovacs, you won't believe what you're gonna see."

Kovacs nodded. He gestured to Carlos to lead the way. "Ten minutes," he said to his driver. "Stay with the car."

They climbed slowly, but when they reached the roof Kovacs was breathing hard and limping. He looked balefully at the little outdoor cafe with its festive lights. "So they've got a place to sit. Is *that* what you wanted to show me?"

"No no," Carlos whispered. "It's *that!"*

"That's a pigeon coop."

"Yeah, but it's what's *inside!"*

"Carlos, there's junk inside. It's a pigeon coop full of junk."

"That's what it looks like, but watch this!" Carlos picked up a piece of brick and lobbed it into the coop. It crashed into the pots and pans.

Silence.

He crept close enough to kick one of the uprights, and then dashed back.

Nothing.

He picked up a length of two-by-four and rammed it into the pile.

No reaction.

"Carlos, did you bring me up here to watch you attack a pigeon coop? To watch you frighten *pots?"*

"Not pots, man. No." Carlos was sweating profusely now. He was wild-eyed and shaking. His binoculars swung against his chest as he waved his arms. "There are flying . . . there are *ghosts* in there, man! Yeah, ghosts!"

Kovacs gazed thoughtfully at him, then headed for the stairs. "See a doctor, Carlos."

"You think I'm crazy?"

"Yes."

"I'm not crazy, Mr. Kovacs. I'm not!"

"Show me. Do your job." Kovacs had reached the third floor.

"Okay. I will. But you gotta give me a little time. Tell Mr. Lacey . . ."

"I'll tell Mr. Lacey *nothing.* You've *had* your time."

Kovacs was on the second floor, headed down. Carlos scampered behind.

"Look, how many jobs like this have I done for you?"

"Six. Seven."

"Always good, eh? You always been satisfied?"

"That was then, this is now." Kovacs strode through the vestibule, out the front door.

"You gotta give me a break, Mr. Kovacs!"

"Wrong." Kovacs got into his car and slammed the door. "Office," he said to his driver.

"Okay, I'll do it!" Carlos shouted as the limo pulled away. "I'll do it *myself!* You wait and see."

In that instant, standing alone on the sidewalk in front of Rileys' Cafe, Carlos Chavez was a little boy again, and everything was larger than he was. His whole world receded with that limousine, and he was left in a cold and hostile place. In that terrible moment, Carlos Chavez, once leader of the Crusaders, thought he was about to cry.

"Bobby!"

Faye. She burst out of the cafe, arms wide to embrace him.

"Hey, lady, my name's not . . ."

"You silly boy! Come in here, now, and have your breakfast."

Frank rushed out after her, glancing nervously at Carlos. "Faye, he's not . . ."

"Look at him, Frank! He's hungry. Now don't *start* at him." She hooked her arm through Carlos's, and before he knew it they were through the door and inside the cafe. "You sit down right over there. We'll have something hot for you in no time."

"Glad you've come," Frank growled at him, too low for Faye to hear. "I got something that belongs to you. Some money."

A quartet of hard hats at a table near the door grinned at Carlos's arrival and called cheerful greetings.

"Hey, it's the enforcer!"

"In for a little warm milk, Carlos?"

"Whatd'ya say, Carlos? Mugged any pregnant women today?"

"Say, Carlos, where's that nice little earring? The one you used to wear right here?"

There was a burst of raucous laughter and shoulder slapping.

"You guys," Carlos said, pointing, "you guys are in trouble! Deep, deep trouble! When I tell Mr. Lacey where you were havin' lunch . . ."

"Right, right, you tell 'im, Carlos. Thing is, we don't work for Lacey. So you go squeal, Carlos. You go tell the teacher! You know what'll happen? Nada. Zip."

Another burst of mocking laughter. More boisterous slapping.

Carlos turned his back on his tormentors. He was sitting at his table with his head in his hands when Faye brought him a huge plate of scrambled eggs, and ham, and home fries, and toast.

"You boys friends of Bobby's?" she asked, smiling sweetly. "You want to stay overnight? Watch TV? Make some peanut butter sandwiches?"

"Uh, no thanks, Mrs. Riley." They turned back to finish their lunch.

"You look awful," Faye said, sitting down beside Carlos as he began to eat. "Thin. Nervous. You know, your father's worried about you, and so am I."

"I don't know nothin' about my father."

"Nonsense! He loves you, Bobby. You know that."

"Look," Carlos said, eating, "I am not who you think I am."

Faye smiled. She looked at the table. She put her arm around him. "Oh, I know mothers don't know everything. I know you have to have your privacy, a life of your own. But just remember where home is. Okay?"

Carlos stopped eating. He laid his fork on the plate. "You people. You know, I really don't want to hurt you people."

"Why *of course* you don't!"

"But I've got a job to do. For Mr. Lacey."

Faye frowned. "He's not a nice man, Bobby. You should find another line of work."

"Maybe I should. But for now he calls the shots. And I'm learning! I'm learning how the city works."

Carlos hesitated. He looked closely at her. "Mr. Lacey's my way outta here, you see? I do a good job for him, I get promoted. Sent somewhere else."

"And then?"

"And then, and then I'm on my way!"

"Where to?"

"Anywhere. See, I'm too smart for this roach trap, this neighborhood."

"Oh, I know you are!"

"I'm intelligent."

"I know that."

"Talented. I've got what it takes to go straight to the top."

"Of course you do! You will! Eat your eggs, now."

Carlos ate, glancing occasionally at the old lady who sat with her chin in her hands, watching him.

"Want some catsup? More coffee?"

It was a good breakfast. He couldn't remember when he

had enjoyed a breakfast like that. He smiled hesitantly at Faye. For a weird moment he almost wished that he *were* her Bobby. He envied him, being able to sit in the cafe like this, every day of his life, talking things over. He suddenly had a tremendous urge to confide in her, but he didn't know how to begin. "I . . . I got feelings, you know," he said.

"Why, of course you do!" Faye laid her hand on his.

"Yeah. I feel bad about some things. Things I gotta do. I don't like . . ." *Hurting people,* he was about to say. *Breaking things up.* But he never had a chance. At that moment a tray of buns floated in from the kitchen.

"Oh, not in here, honey," Faye said. "Back inside. On the counter."

The tray drifted out again.

"Wait a minute!" Carlos was on his feet, pulling his arm out of her grasp. "What the hell was that?"

"Oh, just one of the little guys."

"What *little guys?* You mean those . . ."

"My munchkins. You know, my helpers. Part of the family. Like you. There's another one." She pointed. A cook's puffy, tall white cap sailed out through the serving window, bowed to Carlos, and returned to the kitchen. Faye laughed delightedly. "Clowns. That'll be one of the new ones. Probably Jetsam. Just arrived last night."

Carlos looked wild-eyed around the room, but no one else seemed to have noticed. Everyone was eating and talking normally. He backed towards the door, staring at Faye. "Crazy!" he said, nodding as if understanding something for the first time. "I used to think you were crazy, but it's not that, is it? It's . . . it's *something else!*"

"Oh, yes!" Faye exclaimed, smiling benignly. "It *is* something else." Behind her, two bagels came out of the kitchen and swayed to a few upbeat bars of "Moonglow" before swooping back through the serving window.

Carlos made a strangled noise in his throat.

He staggered backwards through the door of Rileys' Cafe.

He ran.

10 _____

HARRY TRIED EVERYTHING.

After carrying the little stillborn saucer downstairs to his apartment, he had talked to it, shaken it gently, and given it further jolts from a six-volt battery on his workbench. Nothing worked. He had even pried open two of its hatches with tiny screwdrivers and peered inside through a magnifying glass. What he saw was far too complex for him, although one thing was certain: there was no place for batteries. He shook his head. Everything looked so *neat,* so compact, so *right.*

"What's the matter with you, little guy?" Carefully he fastened the hatches back in place. "You ain't dead. I *know* you ain't dead. You just waitin' to be *born.* And old Harry just hasn't got the magic touch." He stared into the little saucer's doleful and lifeless eyes. "We don't need a mechanic here, right? What we need here is a miracle!"

And then, Harry Noble caused the miracle to happen.

Sighing, he leaned back and heaved his boots onto the workbench. Dry wood cracked. Loose nails let go. One of the boards, the one on which the little saucer rested, flipped up, sending the toylike creature spinning into the shelf above the sink. A large open bottle of bleach toppled over, knocking other soaps and fluids into Harry's soaking laundry. The saucer vanished into this seething brew, and an electric clock tipped after it, short-circuiting with enough force to churn the shirts like monstrous sea creatures.

Harry was up and halfway to the sink when the plug shot spinning three feet into the air, and the swirling mixture suddenly drained away, leaving one ruined clock, two shirts, and a pair of trousers, all gleaming white. He poked at these with a wooden spoon. "Hey, little guy! You in there? Where are you?" One after the other he fished the garments out and shook them. No sign of the saucer. There was only the sink, cleaner than it had ever been, and the yawning, old-fashioned drain hole in the center. "Gone!" Harry said. "Down the hole! Poor little fella never had a chance!" Shaking his head, he bent to pick up the workbench board, but when he touched it, he felt it trembling as if alive, and from underneath came a vibrant, high-pitched whine.

Harry frequently heard odd sounds, especially during moments of stress. Sometimes he heard voices, too, and often laughter. But this whining was soon joined by a small clinking like nothing he had ever heard before. It sounded like a fly tapping against a window or a lampshade. He leaned close. He struck his temple with the heel of his hand.

But the sound was not in his head at all. It was real.

It was in the big old drainpipe, and it was moving away fast, under the floor, then through a connection and up one of the exposed pipes near the door. "Hey!" Harry shouted, rushing over and grabbing the pipe.

Something clattered on the inside of the pipe where Harry's hands enclosed it. The whine increased in pitch.

"Stay there!" He ran to his workbench for a pipe wrench, but the sound was already going up and away, out into the hall and along the overhead pipe towards the furnace room. Gripping his wrench, Harry chased it until he lost it in the maze of pipes in the ancient furnace room. "Oh, no!" He grabbed first one pipe and then another, chasing the sound. "Stay still! I'll get you out, but you gotta stay still!"

The sound stopped.

Harry stopped too, listening, mouth open. There were many other small noises. There was the sound of his heart, and the rumble of front-end loaders next door, and a distant burst of laughter from the cafe, and a multitude of creaks and groans vibrating down' the pipes as the old building warmed in the sun.

And there was a burplike gurgle, like a bubble breaking the surface.

And a clink: metal on porcelain.

And a bump: metal on wood.

Cautiously, Harry approached a cubicle in a corner of the furnace room—a caretaker's washroom, unused for many years. When he pulled, the door creaked back on one rusty hinge. There was a dirty old sink, a toilet ... and a bedraggled but bright-eyed little saucer perched on the seat.

"Hey!" Harry shouted, dropping his wrench and throwing up his arms in victory. "You did it!"

The little saucer rose, executed an intricate series of aerobatics, and landed on Harry's outstretched palm, chirping happily. "Weeeems ..." it said. *"Wee*eems ..."

The big man laughed joyously. "Weems, eh? Well, how *are* ya? I'm Harry."

It had been a long, long time since Harry Noble had been happy. He could not remember when. He thought he might have been happy when he was a child with his mother. And he could remember being happy with pets. He had had a cat once, but it disappeared, and once he had had a dog, but it got killed by a truck. He could remember crying, but he could not remember whether that was last year, or the year before, or, maybe, twenty years ago . . .

But that afternoon Harry was happy. The first thing he did was carry Weems back to his room and put him down with infinite care on the counter beside the electrical outlet. Sure enough, a tiny hatch opened, a tiny plug appeared. The saucer hummed contentedly, gazing at Harry.

All that afternoon, Weems followed Harry around the basement rooms, watching closely everything he did, hovering attentively every time he spoke. By nightfall he could do all the tasks that Harry had taught him, and when Harry went to bed, he settled down on the counter near the outlet, small eyes alert.

Harry had not been so happy since his dog, Clancy, had been alive. He dreamed dreams that were so delightful he woke up laughing. In the morning he felt fresh and vigorous, as if all his joints were packed with little sponges, as if he could do five miles of roadwork before breakfast. Even before he got up, he knew that something was different. His small room had been changed during the night. For one thing, it smelled fresh and clean—of detergents, and wax, and linseed soap. For another, it was brighter. Even the ceiling had been magically cleaned and restored, all its stains and cracks removed.

Something was beeping like a small and insistent alarm clock.

Harry sat up.

Perched on the end of his bed was Weems. He was bright-eyed. He beeped happily. He was ready to go.

With his arms full of shopping bags, Mason had trouble fitting the key into the lock of the front door and pushing his way inside. He climbed the stairs two at a time and tapped with the side of his foot on Marisa's door.

"Who is it?"

"It's me. Mason."

"What do you want?"

"Let me in. I've got something for you. I've been doing healthy-baby research."

"Not now, Mason."

"Yes, now! Come on, Marisa, this is exciting. You'll love it! Art meets science! Neo-realism meets nutrition!"

When she opened the door, he gave himself a little trumpet fanfare. "Da-*dah!* It is I, Mason Baylor, nourisher of babies! One side, madam, if you please." He marched past her into the kitchen, deposited his bags on the table, and began to pull out various containers. "Wheat germ, wheat bread, wheatina. Lots of fiber. Milk—whole fat, half-fat, no-fat. Baby book! Fully illustrated, see? Very important!"

"Mason, what are you *doing?* You don't have to take care of me."

"Maybe I don't have to, but I want to, okay? Please." He touched her shoulders. "No obligation."

"Well, Hector . . ."

"Besides, I had fun. From now on, I want to do all the shopping *and* all the research. But there are some things you have to decide pretty soon. Like, for example, do you want Huggies or Pampers? And did you know that there are good substitutes for talcum powder? No zinc."

"Zinc . . . ?"

"Yeah!" Laughing, Mason bent down and waved at Marisa's belly. "Hello in there! Hi! Listen, I just want you to know that when you decide to come out, you'll be coming into a terrific place. This is a house of little miracles! Have we got toys for *you!* They fly! They fix! They don't need any winding."

Marisa began to laugh, hands cradling her stomach.

"Listen, when you decide to come out, you are going to arrive among *friends*. No hostile world for you, no, sir! We are going to . . ."

Mason had dropped to his knees, and as he spoke, his gaze drifted past Marisa, towards the living room. He saw the paintings. His paintings. Everything he had hurled through the window and thought gone forever, mangled under truck tires, burned in oil drums by shivering derelicts.

He stood up very slowly. He looked at Marisa, at the paintings, at Marisa.

"So," she said, shrugging. "I'm a collector. New guy. I just . . . like his work. So, I just . . . pick it up wherever I find it." She blushed. "How d'you like it?"

"I . . . don't know."

"It's my gallery. A one-man show."

"But . . . *why!*"

"I told you. I like it."

Mason brushed the hair out of his eyes. "Well, you asked me what I think. I think maybe you don't know very much about art."

"Maybe." She shrugged. "But then again, maybe I have excellent taste!"

"Pamela . . ."

"Oh, Pamela!" Marisa's eyes flashed. "Don't talk to me about Pamela! She didn't love you. She just *used* you!"

Mason was staring at her, smiling incredulously. "I didn't know you even *knew* Pamela."

"I knew her. I mean, I knew who she was. I could hear..." She blushed and glanced at the ceiling. "It's very thin."

"I see."

"I couldn't help it. When she shouted at you, I just... heard."

Mason was going from one painting to the next. "You really *like* these?"

"Oh, yes! Some of them are, well, gloomy, but that's the way it is, right?"

Mason nodded slowly.

"That doesn't mean it *always* has to be that way. They're true, that's the main thing. They have *heart*."

"This one, now," Mason asked, gesturing to a dark and contorted self-portrait on the mantel. "What does that say to you?"

"That's my favorite. It's a guy standing in the sun."

Mason laughed. "But there *isn't* any sun."

"Yes, there is. We're just not seeing it, because *he* doesn't see it. If he moved two steps in any direction, he'd be in sunshine!" She crossed the room and stood beside him, her eyes shining as she looked at the painting. "You have to keep looking, don't you? You can't see everything at once with art. You have to live with it." She flushed. "Wha... what is it?"

"You. You're very beautiful."

"I'll bet you say that to all pregnant women."

"No."

"I'm fat."

"It doesn't matter."

"Look, I have zits."

"They'll go away."

"My hair's a rat's nest."

"I want to paint you."

Marisa laughed.

"I'm serious," he said. "Will you be my model?"

"When?"

"Now. Right now."

He took her arm and helped her upstairs to his studio. They weren't alone. Flotsam and Jetsam were happily duelling with a pair of brushes, buzzing around at shoulder height. "You guys," Mason said, pointing at them. "Take it easy! I'm gonna need those brushes."

He sat Marisa on a stool, positioned the lights, put on his painting cap, and went to work. Occasionally the saucers drifted by, checking progress. Once, Flotsam altered a line. "Cut it out!" Mason said. "Shoo!" But when he looked at the change, he saw that it was, in fact, not bad. "Thanks!" he called after the little saucer, who was doing loops and victory rolls, chirping ecstatically. "But don't do it again! You do your work, I'll do mine. Okay?"

After an hour Marisa had grown uncomfortable, and Mason helped her down. Her eyes bright as a child's, she asked, "Can I *see* it?"

"Sure. Of course, it's just a sketch. It's not . . ."

But as she approached the easel, a four-note car horn blared through the window, followed by screeching brakes, and laughter, and a wild burst of Latino music.

Marisa's hand went to her mouth. *"Hector!"* She reached as if to touch Mason's face, but then turned and ran downstairs.

"Hector?" Mason called after her. *"Hector?"* He rushed over to the window and looked out. A convertible with a trailer had pulled into the curb, and half a dozen laughing bandsmen were piling out, playing their instruments as they trooped through the vestibule and upstairs to Marisa's apartment.

Hector! Mason had forgotten all about him. The possibility that he should ever return had been so remote, so improbable. But now here he was, disrupting Mason's painting with his blaring horn, shattering the peace of Mason's evening with his exuberant music, destroying Mason's hopes and plans with a single burst of laughter, a single shout for Marisa.

"Hector!" Mason slumped down on the stool. He tossed his brush onto the tray of the easel. He stared morosely at the open door through which Marisa had vanished, and then at the half-finished painting, a strong rendering of Marisa, nude. "Best thing I've ever done, and she didn't even look at it!"

Late into that night the party flourished in Marisa's apartment. At one point, Hector came up and introduced himself, and invited Mason to join them. He went down for a little while, long enough to meet everyone in the band and to have a beer. But then, when the softer music began, and Hector began to sing to Marisa, Mason Baylor said goodnight and left inconspicuously. He went downstairs and out into the warm night, crossing the street and walking a few hundred yards into the Lacey Plaza site. He leaned against a hoarding and looked back at the building.

He thought he had gone far enough to escape Hector's music, but he could still hear it faintly, drifting through one of the two lighted windows on the third floor. Light came from Harry's room in the basement, too, and from the kitchen of Rileys' Cafe, where Frank was baking pies for tomorrow's customers, and from the Rileys' second-floor apartment, where Faye slowly turned the pages of her scrapbook. The vestibule too was brightly lighted once again, after years of broken fixtures, and on the roof the wreath of Christmas lights winked gaily.

The old building was beautiful in the darkness, like a ship serenely voyaging, like an organism composed of many living parts.

Several clear bars of a Spanish serenade drifted across on the breeze, and Mason Baylor turned and walked away, angling across the construction site until he reached the sidewalk.

He kept going.

"Lacey," Carlos said suddenly. He nodded. He finished his coffee and got dressed.

An hour later, nattily garbed in a suit and tie, he entered the foyer of Lacey Inc. He had intended to be earnest and businesslike, projecting an image of cool self-assurance. But he was nervous from the time he arrived. Everything about the place made him nervous. It was all steel and marble and mirrored glass. Sounds echoed in its lobby. Elevators hissed. Fixtures glittered. It was as cold, and impersonal, and functional a building as Carlos had ever seen. It was a building without a *soul*.

Clearly other people felt that way, too. There was no smiling in the reception hall of Lacey Inc., no shouted greetings, no joking. People clicked past each other as if they were on personal conveyor belts, bound for more important places.

A receptionist fixed him with a bland gaze as he approached her desk. "Yes?"

"Hi there!"

She nodded coolly. "May I help you?"

"Want to see Mr. Lacey, please."

"Your name?"

"Carlos."

"Do you have an appointment, Mr. Carlos?"

"No, see, Carlos is the first name. Last name, Chavez."

"I see. And *do* you have an appointment, Mr. Chavez?"

"Well, no."

"I'm afraid Mr. Lacey has no time this morning." Her phone rang, and she answered it, making notes and saying, "Yes, yes, of course," several times before she hung up.

Carlos turned in a little circle of frustration, cracking his knuckles. People in shoes with pointed heels clicked by him.

"Kovacs, then!" he said when she had hung up.

"Mr. Kovacs is also very. . ."

"Just call him," Carlos said softly, leaning close. "Tell him I'm here." And something in his voice caused her to pick up the phone and touch a button.

"There's a Mr. Chavez here to see Mr. Kovacs," she said. "No, a Mr. *Carlos* Chavez."

"He'll be down in a moment," she said, hanging up. "Please clip this name tag to your jacket and take a seat." She pointed with a silver pen.

But Carlos did not take a seat. Instead, he crossed the waiting room to where a six-foot table held a model of Lacey Plaza. There were all the towers of the finished development with their stainless steel and mirrored walls, soaring so high above Carlos's old neighborhood that they had nothing to reflect anymore, except the sky. Carlos bent down until he could see his face in the side of one of the model buildings. It was broken into a score of little square fragments.

"What are *you* doing here?"

He straightened, whirling around. Kovacs had come up behind him. He was accompanied by a cadaverous man in an ash-gray business suit. The man was smoking, smiling at Carlos through the smoke.

"Well?" Kovacs asked again. "Why are you here?"

"I came to see Mr. Lacey."

Kovacs held his hands as if he were about to pass an invisible basketball. "Carlos, I told you, our relationship is at an end. Game over. You are history. Mr. DeWitt here will be looking after 817 East Ninth for us."

"I want to see Lacey."

"Too late. Mr. Lacey does not have time for you, and neither do I. Now, are you going to leave quietly or..."

But at that moment, a small group of executives approached, coming out of a meeting to refer to the model. All wore suits and sober ties, like uniforms—all but Lacey, who was in the center of the group. He was dressed in a very expensive shirt and sweater, and very expensive slacks. His shoes did not click on the marble floor; they were very soft and made no sound at all. One hand was in his pocket. From the other dangled a little string of beads that he toyed with as he talked. They made a sound like small teeth snapping. He regarded Carlos with coolly amused gray eyes. "Who's this?" he asked.

Kovacs and DeWitt moved aside. "Carlos Chavez, Mr. Lacey," Kovacs said. "You remember I told you..."

"I remember very well. You don't look crazy, Carlos."

"Crazy?" Carlos lost control of his laugh, and it went a little shrill. *"I'm* not crazy!"

"Kovacs here says you've been seeing things."

"Well, I can explain that, Mr. Lacey. Thing is..."

"He also says you attacked a—what was it?—a *chicken* coop?"

All the men had begun to smile now, looking at Carlos with interest.

"Well, it was a pigeon coop. You see..."

Lacey closed his eyes. He gestured Carlos away from the model. "Don't know the difference. I'm a vegetarian myself. But I *do* know the difference between this," he indicated the model of Lacey Plaza, "and *this*." He lifted away one of the hollow skyscrapers. Underneath was a perfect replica of 817 East Ninth Street, complete to the last detail, even to the gold lettering on the window of Rileys' Cafe.

"Mr. Lacey, I *gave* them the money!"

"Why aren't they gone, Carlos?"

"They *will* be gone. I promise. I just need a bit of time."

One of the group looked at his watch. Two others began to discuss quietly some detail in the model.

"Time is something I don't have. Neither do you. In a day, permits for that property expire. Options vanish."

"I know about options! Lot assembly! Unencumbered parcels! I been learning, Mr. Lacey!"

"Good for you. Maybe you'll have a career in real estate. Maybe in Nebraska." He replaced the shell of the building. Blue suits moved between him and Carlos.

"History," Kovacs said, making his basketball gesture again.

Carlos backed towards the revolving doors. "I'm gonna do it for you, Mr. Kovacs. You'll see! Tonight! By tonight they'll be gone!"

Kovacs winked. "If I were you, I'd just stay away, Carlos. I told you, Mr. DeWitt here is looking after things for us now."

The thin man with Kovacs smiled. He had a gold tooth that glinted at Carlos like a little stab of lightning.

11 _____

AND SO, THE end of 817 East Ninth began.

Later, when he talked about it, Frank would shake his head ruefully and remark on the ironic twists and surprises that life held in store: "There's an old saying that the night is darkest just before the dawn. But you know what I've noticed? I've noticed that sometimes the opposite's true. Sometimes, just when you think everything's perfect, everything's on the upswing—bam!—that's when you get hit! Disaster! So there we were . . ."

There they were. They had had another busy day. It had gone so well that Frank had even given a kid a free soda to run over to the smoke shop and buy him a very good cigar, which he had carried in his shirt pocket for hours, taking it out occasionally just to savor it and anticipate it. It had gone so well that by the time they closed, Faye was exhausted, but her eyes were bright, and she was laughing happily, and she looked younger than Frank had seen her look for a long, long time.

"Let's dance!" she said.

Frank waved towards an empty table. "In a minute. In a minute. Let's just take a little break first."

Like a dignified butler, Pa floated out of the kitchen and across the cafe to the front door. He extended a silver gripper and turned the red cardboard sign from OPEN to CLOSED. He drew down the blind. He turned the key. He switched off the lights beside the front windows. And then, as Frank and Faye settled down in their seats, he brought out a cup of chocolate for Faye. Frank clipped the end of the Havana, and as he put the cigar into his mouth and started patting his pockets for matches, the saucer hovered, opened a small hatch, and shot out a laserlike beam that set the end of the cigar glowing.

Frank laughed. "Thanks, pal," he said.

"To you," Faye said, and raised her cup of chocolate.

And that was where they were and what they were doing when, suddenly, the building went dark.

Harry was in the hall when the lights went out. He had spent the day happily teaching Weems how to cook, how to clean up, how to wash and iron, how to darn socks and mend frayed shirts.

Try as he might, however, Harry could not coax Weems into his pocket. He wanted to carry him around there, as he had carried his hamster, Murphy, when he was a kid. But the little saucer was wary. He flew close, he peered inside, but he wouldn't go in. He preferred space and freedom. He preferred zipping exuberantly around the room whenever he wished, turning loops and somersaults, beeping happily.

Then, as Harry was getting ready for bed, similar beepings came from the hall. There were two tones, one like high laughter, one lower, more annoyed. A chase! They were past Harry's door and gone in a moment, but Weems heard them. Frantically, he swooped into the bathroom where Harry was brushing his teeth and tugged on his shirt with a silvery gripper.

"What?" Harry asked. "Whatsamatter?"

He let himself be led to the door, where the little saucer flitted back and forth, now grappling helplessly with the knob, now hovering in front of Harry, beeping and pointing.

"You . . . you wanna *go?*"

Much excitement, nodding, flapping of grippers.

Harry shuffled to the door. He hesitated. "Well, okay, little guy, if you wanna go. I'm not gonna keep you prisoner. Just remember . . ."

But when he had opened the door and Weems had zipped through into the hall, he was astonished to find him coming back, beckoning to him. "Hey! You want me to come *with* you? Okay!"

They raced down the hall and up the stairs, Harry moving well for such a large man, as if his old footwork had been restored to him, and he was the Harry Noble of years ago, whom crowds had cheered. When they reached the stairwell, Weems shot straight up. Harry followed, taking the stairs two at a time. At the main floor he heard a jubilant chorus of hums and beeps and birdlike greetings above.

He looked up.

Circling, soaring, diving, their lights slicing weirdly through the dim space two floors above, Ma, Pa, Flotsam, and Jetsam were welcoming Weems as he rose toward them. While the others continued to frolic, Ma drifted gently down to embrace her small, miraculously restored offspring, and the two of them performed a rocking little dance that was not, after all, much unlike the moving embraces Harry had seen at bus stations between relatives who had thought themselves separated forever.

Beaming, Harry shielded his eyes to see better, and he was so absorbed he did not even realize when all the lights went out. He heard Frank coming down the hall from the door of the cafe saying, "Hey, Harry, what happened?" and he lowered his hands to see that, except for the pale beam of Frank's flashlight, he was standing in total darkness.

When the lights went out, Mason, a bit drunk and more than a bit astonished, was standing with Marisa in his arms.

He had come back from the bar only a short time before to find Hector's red convertible and trailer gone, and when he climbed the stairs and found the door to Marisa's apartment open and no one inside, he nodded bitterly; she had gone with Hector. He leaned in and switched on a light. She had left all her furniture—and, of course, his paintings, the paintings she had claimed to like so much. He laughed bitterly. She had abandoned them, just as she had abandoned him.

Mason Baylor was not a violent man, but at that moment such despondency flooded him that he feared he might weep. Instead, he strode into the room and kicked a painting that was leaning against the wall, smashing the frame to splinters, crumpling the canvas, and hurling the wreckage against the opposite wall. He did not feel better; he felt worse—emptier, stupider, angrier. He was just picking up a chair to hit the next canvas when he heard his name from the doorway behind him.

"Mason! What are you *doing?* Stop it! Those are *mine!*"

"Marisa?"

"Of course, Marisa. Put my chair down!" She swept

past him and wrung her hands over the ruined painting. "Oh, look what you've done!"

"Marisa, where *were* you?"

"In your apartment."

"But why?"

"Well, I thought you might want... I thought you might want to finish my painting." She blushed.

"But where's Hector?"

"He's on his way to Chicago, with the band."

"He *left* you? That son of a bitch!"

"I told him to go. It's a break for him, really, a very big job."

"But what about the baby?"

Marisa bit her lip. She clasped her hands nervously. "Well, I thought... I mean, I know there are places that would help us—agencies, places like that. But I thought, well, you seemed to be interested, Mason. In the *baby*, I mean. You seemed to want to *do* things for it. And..." Suddenly she looked up at him, tears brimming. "And besides, I think... I think I love you."

Mason spoke her name. He said it several times as she came into his arms, and several more times against her hair, against the place where her neck and shoulder met.

His eyes were closed, as were hers, and so for a few moments neither of them knew that the lights had gone out.

The lights went out because Carlos Chavez chopped the wires.

It was so simple, really, that he wondered why he hadn't thought of it before. He laughed. His laughter was a little high, a little mechanical, like the squeaking of a rusty door.

Near midnight, when the residents of 817 East Ninth all seemed to be preoccupied, Carlos crept along the edge of the construction site and crossed the darkened street. He was no longer wearing his suit. He had changed into cast-off fatigues and sneakers, and he was carrying a stolen fire-axe. He pried up the grating in the window well of the furnace room. He looked furtively around, slipped through the opening, and lowered the grating softly behind him. With a few light blows he chopped through the window screen and jimmied the sash. The old window rose grudgingly, but soon he could squeeze through and drop inside.

Enough dim light glimmered in the furnace room for him to pick his way soundlessly through the litter on the floor across to the water main. Here he braced himself, swung the axe high, and struck savagely again and again, as if the old pipe were everything that had gone wrong, everything he did not understand, everything mocking him. In seconds he was drenched by gushing water as the smashed joint burst.

The fuse box now! He found it on the opposite wall, short-circuited by an old trowel. With a single blow he severed the trunk lines, showering himself with sparks. Again he struck savagely and repeatedly, venting rage.

He was still flailing when the door opened and a beam of light probed down the steps. "Hey!" a voice said. "Who's that?"

Carlos whirled, cursing.

Frank was coming in with his flashlight. Behind him Harry loomed unnaturally huge in the weird light, and around Harry's head glowed what looked to Carlos like several pairs of enormous, round eyes.

Carlos brandished his axe. "Get back!" he shouted over the rushing water.

After that, things happened very fast. The big saucers

left the little ones perched on Harry's arm and zoomed into the furnace room.

Disoriented, drenched by spraying water and pinned like a bug by the beam of Frank's flashlight, Carlos saw only two huge pairs of red eyes, hurtling at him.

He screamed. He flailed blindly with the axe, catching Pa squarely on the back, cutting him almost in half. Pieces scattered. He crashed to the concrete floor and spun helplessly, uttering a dying whine. His lights, one pointed at Carlos and the other at the ceiling, went dim, went gray, went black.

Ma shrieked. Her normal, persistent whine suddenly rose to an ear-piercing squeal, so awful that it rooted the humans where they stood. She flooded the room with a dazzling fluorescence, like a hundred synchronized flashguns, and everyone saw everything at once in stark black and white, like a freeze-frame in a movie. They saw Frank, gaping in horror, holding his flashlight, and Harry with the three small saucers perched like frightened birds on his arm, and Carlos staring at the mangled chunk of metal that had been Pa.

Mason Baylor, artist, gentle man of peace, said, "You murdering son of a bitch!" and picked up a length of two-inch pipe.

Holding Carlos in the beam of his light, Frank groped into the coal bin and found a shovel he had not touched since 1948.

All three baby saucers sprang off Harry's arm and fled into the darkness, beeping frantically.

Ma lunged at Carlos, clouting him hard on the side of the head, sending him reeling against the furnace. His axe clattered on the ducts as he swung wildly. Ma circled so fast she was just a blur streaking at Carlos, but this time she bounced off the axe handle as Carlos swung again. She hit the wall and spun out of control to the floor near her mate. She whimpered. She crawled closer to Pa. She reached out with tiny grippers to touch him.

Carlos leapt towards her with the axe raised. He was snarling. Blood streamed from a cut over his right eye. In another instant Ma too would have been destroyed, but Mason Baylor stepped over both her and her shattered mate. He raised his length of pipe. He spoke two words through clenched teeth: "Get out!"

Carlos whirled and ran for the door, ramming the butt of the axe into Harry Noble's midsection. "Out of my way!" he shouted, shoving Marisa and Faye aside.

Marisa gasped and cried out, staggering back against the wall, holding her stomach.

"Bobby!" Faye shouted, but Carlos was beyond hearing. He had reached the first-floor corridor. He was running for the door.

Harry followed him. He recovered quickly from the low blow to his stomach and moved deliberately down the hall to his apartment. When he emerged, he was pulling on a pair of huge boxing gloves. He worked his shoulders a little as he walked. He climbed the stairs.

When Carlos reached the front door, he found it jammed.

Afterwards, Frank would ask Mason what he had done to the door when he came home that night, and Mason would swear that he had done nothing at all. The door, he said, had opened normally and shut normally. But the fact was, for whatever reason, that when Carlos tried to escape the door wouldn't let him.

It stayed shut.

Carlos cursed, kicked, twisted the lock and the knob. Nothing happened. He stepped back, swung the fire-axe crashing into the frame, and raised it for another blow.

But Carlos's time in 817 East Ninth had finally run out. On the backswing the axe was snatched out of his hands, and he turned to face Harry, smiling grimly. Behind Harry, down the corridor, the other residents had regrouped and were moving forward.

Carlos spread his hands. He faked a smile. "What's this? You're all together now, huh? That it? Help one, help..." As fast and as hard as he could, he swung at Harry—a right cross and then a left uppercut to the jaw. The big man blocked both blows effortlessly. He sighed. He looked very sad about what must now happen. "Oh, no," he said. "No, no, no."

The first blow landed just below Carlos's chest. It was hard enough to lift him off his feet and send him crashing back against the wall. He doubled over, eyes bulging, knees buckling.

"Bobby!" Faye screamed.

Frank held her. "Faye, honey, it's not Bobby. It's..."

Harry propped Carlos up with one hand, shifting him so that his back was towards the door.

"Hold it! Hold it!" Mason squeezed past them and effortlessly opened the splintered door. He held it with one hand while he cupped the other like a megaphone and shouted into the dark street, "And now, ladees 'n' gennulmun, coming to you from ringside! The thrill and victory, and... oogh!"

He winced as Harry steadied the limp form of Carlos and delivered a terrible right uppercut that lifted him clean off his feet once more and sent him skidding on his rear end through the vestibule and down the front steps to the sidewalk, where he sprawled and lay still, out cold.

"...and the agoneee of defeat!" Mason said, letting the door swing shut. He grabbed Harry's gloved hand and raised it high.

"Bobby! Bobby!"

Frank held Fay's shoulders. "Dammit!" he shouted. "Will you look at me, please? He's not Bobby, Faye! He's just a *punk!* He's somebody who . . ."

But she was twisting free of him, struggling towards the door. "Let me go! He's hurt! What's the *matter* with you!"

Frank blocked her way, forcing her face up so that she had to look at him. "Faye, Bobby's dead. You know that. He's *dead!*"

She recoiled, hands clamped to her ears.

"You *wish* he were dead!" she screamed.

"No, Faye!"

"Yes, you do. You *do!* You hate him!"

Frank looked suddenly much smaller, much grayer. He put a fist in the middle of his chest, as if to keep something together. "No," he said softly, shaking his head. "I never hated him. I loved him."

"All you ever do is yell at him and make him feel he's not good enough. See? You won't even help him when he's hurt. Your own *son*, Frank!" She drew back, blinking, back towards the stairs, back towards the safety of her bedroom with all its albums and smiling faces. "Well, he's . . . he's gone now, isn't he? That's why he bought that car, wasn't it? To get away. To get away from *you*, Frank."

"Faye, don't say that. Please don't."

"It's your fault!"

The old man turned away as if he had been slapped. Mason and Marisa went to him at once. "Frank, she didn't . . ."

"Look after her," he said, his voice choking. "Please take her upstairs and look after her." He patted Marisa's shoulder and turned away towards his darkened cafe, stooped, and old, and terribly hurt, waving one hand absently, as if brushing away some pesky insect.

When he had gone, when Marisa had helped Faye upstairs and Mason and Harry were left alone in the hallway, Mason's eye was caught by a tiny gleam beside the baseboard, and he bent to pick up a silvery facsimile of a human leg, one of the baby saucers'. Farther along, he found another, and then another, until finally he had gathered six. "Human parts," he said, holding them out so Harry could see them. "Jettisoned."

"Know why?" Harry asked. He looked sorrowfully at the big gloves covering his fists. "Know what humans do? Humans kill."

"Damn it!" Mason said. "Why did this have to happen? You think they'll come back, Harry?"

"Would you?" Alone, shoulders sagging, Harry turned and lumbered off down the dark hall like a huge bear.

12 _____

THERE WAS NOTHING to do for the rest of the night but hope. Mason found an old pair of rubber boots and waded through the basement to the shutoff valve to stop the flood. Faye had been given a sedative and sent to sleep with Frank's flashlight glowing beside her bureau. The others gathered in the cafe, huddled around a table with a single candle burning in the center.

"You know," Frank said as Mason rejoined them, "if *they* were here now, if they were still on our side, we wouldn't have a thing to worry about. They'd have this mess cleaned up in no time."

But the saucers had gone. Horrified by what they had seen, the three little ones had zoomed straight through the front window of Rileys' Cafe so fast they had punched three holes without even cracking the glass. Weems had made a small round one; Flotsam, an oval one; Jetsam, one almost perfectly square.

Ma had retreated to the pigeon coop, where she crouched with all her antennae and appendages fully extended, hissing. Before the water reached them, Marisa had gathered up Pa's remains on a large cookie sheet, and carried them as close as she dared to this glowing, bristling creature in the coop. Then she went downstairs to join the others. "She hates us now," she said. "I guess to her we all look like Carlos."

Harry sat unmoving, staring at the three holes in the window. Frank brought him a cup of coffee, but he didn't drink it. Mason tried to comfort him by saying that Weems would return sooner or later, but although Harry nodded, he obviously didn't believe it. About 2 a.m. he got up suddenly and went back downstairs to his soggy room, taking a candle with him. He rummaged through a chest of drawers and found what he was looking for, tucked in behind some shirts, and a yo-yo, and some shriveled chestnuts that had once been brown and gleaming, and a leather bag of marbles, and an India-rubber ball, and a carefully folded punch-out Valentine with I LOVE YOU HARRY NOBLE, CHRISTINE printed on it in pencil.

A dog whistle.

He held it up. It was still as bright as it had been when he used to put it to his lips and blow so hard his eyes went slitty, blow a long and silent high-frequency note that would bring Clancy, his maybe-half Irish setter loping home from whatever alleys and trash cans he was exploring. "Clancy," Harry said, reminiscing for a moment with the whistle in the palm of his massive hand. Then he went upstairs and out into the city night, alone.

In the cafe, Mason put his arm around Marisa. "You okay? That guy shoved you pretty hard."

She nodded.

"Sure? You look pale."

"I'm all right," she said, looking at Frank. The old man sat slumped on his chair, hands hanging between his knees, staring blankly out into the darkness. "She didn't mean it," Marisa said to him. "Faye didn't really mean what she said."

Frank shook his head. "Oh, no, she meant it. She doesn't say it often, about twice a year, maybe, but she meant it. It's as close as she ever comes to telling the truth about Bobby."

Mason asked. "What *is* the truth, Frank?"

"Bobby? He bought a car. He went for a drive. A drunk hit him head-on. It was the first time. First time he ever drove his car. First and last."

"H-how long ago?"

"Nineteen years, seven months, fourteen days."

"And she's been . . ."

"Yeah, Faye just refused to admit it, although she knows the truth deep down. She just has to pretend that he'll come home someday. Has to keep looking for him. You know, the funny thing is that she's been happier ever since these little guys came." He shrugged and laughed. "How do you explain that? Something unreal happens, and Faye gets more in touch with reality. Now, this. Just when I thought maybe . . ." He gestured to the three holes in the window, and to the darkness of the city into which the little saucers had fled.

Mason shrugged gloomily, staring through the holes and out into the night. He felt empty. Carlos may have lost a fight, but he had won the war as far as Mason could see. They had no water, no power, no future. The best thing, the sensible thing, would be to pack up right then and get out. He turned to Marisa to suggest this, but when he saw her with her arms wrapped around the child in her womb, when he saw her staring into space and biting her lip to keep back the tears, Mason Baylor suddenly did not feel like giving up. He did not feel like running. He felt like fighting back.

"To hell with it!" he said, slapping his knees and standing up. "We're gonna keep this family together! You two wait here. I'll be back when I've found those little guys!"

Where had they gone?

Into the city, that was all the humans knew. How far they went, or how fast, or what their route was, no one would ever know.

Many night people saw them. A cook in a twenty-four-hour restaurant, stepping outside for a breath of air, was suddenly frozen by three saucerlike objects swooping around the cowl of a futuristic street light. "Hey!" he yelled. Three pairs of luminous, hovering eyes regarded him . . . and vanished.

Later he said to his assistant, "Joey, you ever seen anything funny?"

"Sure! Let's see, I seen the Marx Brothers in *Monkey Business*, I seen Charlie Chaplin in *Hard Times*, I seen Woody Allen . . ."

"I mean *funny*. Odd, peculiar, strange."

"I seen the guy my sister married!"

"No. Something you didn't understand. You know, like, a flying saucer, for example."

"Never. You wanna know what I think about stuff like that?"

"Yeah."

"It ain't *out there*. It's *in here*. Right between the ears."

A cable-TV serviceman saw them.

He was driving a van with a dish antenna on the roof. Suddenly streaks of light zipped past his windows, crisscrossing, swooping back. He braked and pulled into the curb. Three round, bright pairs of eyes peered through his windshield.

He tried to smile. He waved.

For a moment the eyes regarded him. Then they were gone—straight up.

He clicked on the receiver in the back of the van, sending the dish antenna tilting, sweeping the sky, and through his headphone he heard a sound, like small birds moving away at high speed.

He picked up the microphone of the two-way radio. "Sammy? Bruno. Do me a favor. It's a little unusual. Just humor me. I want you to call the Air Force and ask them . . . ready for this, Sammy? Ask them if they have . . ."

The driver of a street sweeper saw them.

It was a very large and powerful sweeper, and driving it was such a boring job that the operator often fell asleep and let the roaring monster prowl on its own, nuzzling the curb.

He was dozing that night. The sweeper had rolled through several red lights before an old car roared past, horn blaring. A hubcap spun off its front wheel. The sweeper driver awoke to see a metal disc bounding in front of him.

Hubcap.

Hubcaps were no problem. The machine ate them.

He opened the window to clear his head, and when he looked back, the hubcap was multiplying!

Where there had been only one a moment before, there were now *four* metallic discs, three of them smaller, hovering above the wobbling hubcap and turning to face the sweeper with bright, orange, angry eyes. Whining viciously, one of them clattered against the windshield.

He halted. He reversed, causing a warning beeper to go off in the rear of the machine. Immediately all three saucers swooped towards the sound. The driver watched them in his rearview mirror, whirling briefly around the corner of his vehicle like molecules around the nucleus of an atom. Then they zipped away to the northwest, three narrow bands of light.

Several airport traffic controllers saw the saucers.

They went around the tower windows so fast they were like ribbons tying up a big, round package.

The controllers kept cool. They checked their screens. All aircraft were accounted for, all procedures normal.

Later, during a break, one of them said, "What the hell *was* that?"

"Searchlight?"

"Right around the tower?"

"Something inside. A reflection."

"Uh-unh. There's nothing like that. Nothing."

"An anomaly, then."

"Yeah. An anomaly."

These and many other people saw the small saucers that night, but Mason and Harry searched in vain.

Blowing his whistle, Harry wandered aimlessly through the streets collecting more and more stray dogs, until he ended up in the middle of a happy, gamboling pack sprawled across the entire sidewalk. People squeezed into doorways and ducked into alleys when they saw them coming. Once a police car prowled close, and a voice said over the loud-hailer, "Hey, buddy, what you got I haven't got?"

Harry grinned and waved his whistle over the sea of dogs. "Humane Society," he said. He opened his wallet and showed his birth certificate. "Truck's just around the corner. Up the street."

The police drove off.

Mason searched more methodically. He decided to check every major power outlet within a mile radius. He went first to the local transfer station, keeping his eye on the pylons and the heavy-duty wires all the way there and back. He checked the radio and TV stations. He even checked the third rail at subway stations.

Nothing.

Finally, near dawn, Mason turned towards Times Square and the huge, brightly lit billboards there. If that area of the city drew more wattage per square inch than any other, it might draw the saucers, too. He took a cab, although he couldn't really afford one. After a few blocks the cabbie said, "Hey, buddy, why you got your head out the window that way?"

"Fresh air," Mason said.

The cabbie shook his head. "Get back inside! You want fresh air, go to Nevada."

Harry had arrived in Times Square before him. He was surrounded by dogs, and he was gazing up at a bewildering assortment of blazing signs. Harry stared intently at the largest of these signs, a huge illuminated ellipse advertising pantyhose. It was adorned with several pairs of svelte, bodiless legs, but it was not these that had seized Harry's attention; it was the shape of the sign itself.

Suddenly, an idea formed.

Harry looked around. Behind him, a city maintenance vehicle idled at the curb while two workers swept up litter. The front doors were open. On the seat lay a power megaphone. Harry looked at it. He looked back up at the sign, and then at the megaphone again.

Mason got out of his taxi just in time to see his friend,

surrounded by dogs, race into a building, a megaphone held high. Two men in white coveralls shouted and chased him, until the gamboling dogs swarmed over them.

"Hey! Harry! Wait for me!"

The big man kept going. Once inside the building he headed straight for the stairs and climbed steadily, with the determination of a man who knows where he is going, and why. Even when he got to the roof, he kept going, straight up the ladder that led to the service catwalk for the sign, and then out across the face of the sign itself, past the humming transformers and into the center of the huge parabola. There he clamped the whistle in his lips, raised the megaphone and aimed it up and out over the city, and blew a long and mighty blast.

Humans heard nothing; dogs for miles around began to bark.

Harry blew again.

Mason arrived on the roof to hear Harry shouting excitedly and pointing to the east, towards the first gray streaks of dawn. There, coming rapidly in tight formation, were three unmistakable pairs of small, round lights.

At the first light of dawn, Faye awoke. All night she had had troubled dreams of Bobby and of Frank, of other times and places, of things that had been and things that might have been.

Sometimes when she woke up, she could not remember where she was or even who she was. Slowly, bit by bit, she would then collect enough of herself to function—to get up, and dress, and speak to Frank, and begin the day.

This morning, however, she was wide awake instantly, remembering all the terrible things that had happened the night before. She remembered Carlos destroying Pa; she remembered the fight between Harry and Carlos in the hall;

she remembered Marisa gathering the mangled remains of Pa saucer, while the water rose towards her, and carrying them up to the roof; she remembered Ma, a little nodule of terror and hatred, crouched and bristling in the pigeon coop.

She sat up. She looked through her door and into the living room. Marisa lay curled on the couch with a blanket wrapped around her. Frank was asleep in his chair.

Quietly Faye got up and put on her slippers and dressing gown. Quietly she opened the door and closed it behind her. Quietly she went down the hall and up the stairs to the roof.

It was just daybreak, just light enough to see the gray skyline of the city to the east, and some frail streaks of pink on the undersides of the clouds. The little roof garden, where they had all sat so happily together such a short time before, looked dusty and shabby now in this bleak first light. Bobby's pigeon coop, where they had watched the arrival of the three little saucers, looked ramshackle and abandoned.

But Faye knew that it was not abandoned. Softly in her slippers, she drew close.

Ma had been busy overnight. She still was. An assortment of tiny tools appeared and disappeared in her silver grippers as she probed deep inside Pa's innards. She was so preoccupied that she paid little attention as Faye approached, except to cast one baleful glance in her direction.

Pa was reconstructed! Restored! Except that he was not moving. He showed no vital signs at all. His antennae drooped. His stabilizers hung limp. No light shone from his headlamps or from the many apertures around his rim. He looked like one of Harry's models without batteries. Inert. Earthbound.

As Faye watched, Ma withdrew her gripper from the hatch through which she had been making some adjustment. Two tiny clips went inside and clamped onto terminals Faye could not see. Already plugged into the power cord, Ma braced herself and relayed a jolt that sent Pa vibrating four inches into the air. But when he settled back on the roof he was the same as he had been—lifeless. Again she tried. And again.

No luck.

"Something missing?" Faye asked.

Large eyes regarded her. For several minutes neither moved. The two beings, human and other-than-human, looked at each other for a long, long time. And then one of Ma's grippers extended, shaped into a tiny circle to indicate wire of a certain diameter, and two grippers demonstrated wire of a certain length.

Faye drew out one hairpin and offered it.

A silvery gripper received it. A silvery magnifying glass extended, focused. Swiftly, something intricate happened inside Pa's hatch. Again the electrical clips went back in, clamped, and again a jolt sent Pa shuddering into the air.

But still, no response.

This time, however, Faye got into the act. She stepped into the coop and gave the saucer a firm kick on the rear end with her slippered foot. "Hey!" she said. "Snap out of it!"

It worked. Pa skidded against the chicken wire and shook himself. His eyes blinked open. His rimlights snapped on. His antennae trembled and hummed. His stabilizers spun him around to face Faye.

"Go!" she said. "Don't worry about me! Go look after the little ones before it's too late!"

She backed across the roof as the sun rose behind her, shimmering in her white hair and silhouetting her frail body through the diaphanous gown. She clasped her hands together as the two saucers went airborne and swooped out of the pigeon coop.

"But, please," she whispered, suddenly afraid, "please come back. Don't leave us alone for good!"

Already the saucers were several blocks away. Faye glimpsed two silvery orbs in the rising sun, like eyes blinking. And then, they vanished.

Weems came to Harry immediately and settled on the palm of his large hand, bounding and beeping happily. Flotsam and Jetsam circled once and then attached themselves to the closest transformer, sucking up such vast quantities of juice that the sign went dull.

Beaming, carrying his small friend carefully, Harry picked his way down the rickety steps of the catwalk and rejoined Mason on the roof.

Mason was laughing wildly, clapping him on the back. "Hey, buddy! You did it! You did it!"

So the two adult saucers found him. They came in so fast that the happy men on the roof had no warning. There was a sound like silk tearing, keen edges slicing air, and then two hollow pops, like a double-barreled shotgun, as they decelerated to sonic speed and rose, glinting silver discs in the new sun. They halted, spun, came back. Ma summoned her offspring away from the transformer with a sequence of shrill beeps, and Pa hovered five feet in front of Mason and Harry, eyes bright orange.

"You're back!" Mason said, spreading his arms. "All in one piece!"

Pa stayed where he was. He held his airspace. The color of his eyes shifted from orange to red. A snapping, high-voltage growl came out of him.

"Doesn't trust you," Harry said.

"Me! But it was Carlos who hit him!"

"Same species. Let me talk to him."

Harry stood serenely with his hands cupping Weems, and Pa hovered, rocking a bit, his angry glow undiminished. Ma and the other two slid into formation behind him.

Then, on some signal that Mason couldn't hear, they turned and swept away in tight formation. They went at incredible speed. One minute they were there; the next, gone.

A frantic beeping came out of Harry Noble's clasped hands, but he seemed oblivious to it. "Gone," he said, looking at Mason as if he might cry. "They're gone for good now, aren't they?"

"Let him go, too, Harry."

"Huh?"

Mason pointed to Harry's clasped hands, and the big man stared at them as if they belonged to somebody else, as if the pleading coming out of them had just begun. He opened them, and with a flutter of grateful sounds, Weems zoomed after the others.

"He coulda hurt me," Harry said, "but he didn't. He just . . . asked."

"Harry, I thought you were gonna talk to him. Pa."

"I did."

"But you didn't *say* anything."

Harry shook his head. "There are ways and ways of talkin'."

"What, what did you tell him?"

"I told him we were sorry. I told him to please stay, because there was a lot that needed fixin' in the world, and in us, too."

Mason shrugged. "Didn't work."

"Nope." Harry shook his head sadly and looked off to

the south, where the saucers had vanished. "Didn't work at all."

Mason put his arm around him. "They might come back. You don't know."

Harry kept shaking his head, staring south long after there was nothing to see but the haze and smog of the city, yellowish-gray in the new sun. His cheeks were wet.

13 _____

ALL DAY FAYE stayed in her room with the door closed and the curtains drawn, firmly refusing to go downstairs. "I'm waiting," she said.

Marisa made tea for her and prepared her medicines, moving slowly, resting often. Frank, Harry, and Mason spent the day mopping out the basement and splicing wires. In the evening, when the four of them gathered in the cafe, Mason and Harry sank gratefully into their chairs at the corner table, but Marisa sat down very carefully, on the edge of her chair.

"What is it?" Mason asked. "What's wrong?"

She spread both hands low on her abdomen. "I . . . I have pains."

"What?"

She nodded. "I've had them all day. I thought maybe they were just from all the excitement."

Harry took a sip of coffee and set the cup down softly. "Baby time," he said.

Mason leapt up. "But I *asked* you if you were all right! Hours ago!"

"I was. I am. But . . . *oh!*" She bit her lip and leaned forward.

"Hospital!" Mason shouted. "Cab! We gotta go!" He flew to the telephone.

The taxi was there in minutes, and Mason and Harry helped Marisa into it. Mason climbed in beside her, and Harry was about to follow, but he hesitated, looking doubtfully at Frank and up at the dark windows of the Rileys' apartment. "You gonna be all right, you and Faye?"

"Sure," Frank said. "We're fine. Really. You go ahead. Go *on!*" He leaned down and smiled at Marisa, who looked very small huddled next to the two men. He signaled a *V* for victory. "Have a wonderful baby!"

And then suddenly the cab was gone, and Frank Riley was alone. He strolled a few steps in one direction, a few steps in the other. He stretched. He rubbed his aching back.

"Have a wonderful baby!" That was what Bobby's grandfather, Faye's father, had said to his daughter on this very spot all those years ago as Frank had hurried her off to the hospital. When he had returned later that night with the splendid news that all was well and that they had a son, Faye's father had been waiting, dozing, with cigars and brandy all laid out. There in the cafe, together, they had lit their cigars and raised their glasses to the new life just beginning—Bobby's.

Frank blew his nose.

And now, still, in spite of everything, life was going on, starting fresh. There would soon be a new baby, and two happy young parents, and even when 817 East Ninth was gone and Rileys' Cafe long forgotten, there would be other new beginnings elsewhere, and what he and Faye had been together would be part of those fresh starts.

Frank nodded, shrugged.

You tried, you did your best, you lost some, won some, survived, got old. Sometimes terrible things happened to you, like losing friends forever, and sometimes wonderful things happened, like . . .

"Being a grandfather!" Frank said. He spread his arms. He laughed and patted his vest pocket.

No cigar.

But there *had* to be cigars! Mason and Harry would be coming back, and the three of them would sit in the cafe and celebrate. They would raise a glass of brandy to this wonderful small new life, and they would enjoy together the rich smoke wreathing from good cigars.

Frank hastened back inside, taking off his apron. If Faye was already in bed, he might have time to slip around to the smoke shop.

Sure enough, she was sound asleep.

Frank closed the bedroom door softly. He went back downstairs, and out the front door of the cafe, locking it behind him.

He would be only twenty minutes. Half an hour at most.

From the shadows among the rubble heaps, behind the sign for Lacey Plaza, Marcel DeWitt watched him go. He was smiling thinly in the darkness, revealing his gold tooth. He could not believe his good luck. For two hours he had been waiting, smoking, wondering how to get that building empty so he could go to work. And now, here it was! Empty.

He puffed on his cigarette and then blew on the tip, so that it glowed brightly.

Marcel DeWitt was an arsonist, although he preferred to call himself a pyrotechnician. Tucked into the breast pocket of his suit he had a very thin envelope containing several very large bills, the money Lacey had paid him, through Kovacs, to accidentally and thoroughly burn this irksome little building. In the suitcase-sized metal container beside him, he had everything he needed to do the job.

Marcel DeWitt was happy in his work. All his life he had loved fires and all his life he had lit them. They did not have to be large fires, although occasionally he did love a spectacle, and if something that had started small got big, well, that was just spontaneous combustion. He could not remember wanting to be a pyrotechnician because he could not remember *not* being one, right from the age of six or seven when he had shooed his sister's rabbits out of their hutch and touched a match to the straw inside. To him, fire-making was both craft and art, and as in any art, chance often took a hand to produce divine results.

And he was good, Marcel DeWitt. Very, very good. That was why he had never been convicted. That was why there was a thin envelope of very large bills in his breast pocket as he stood finishing his cigarette, looking at the darkened building that he would soon turn into a spontaneous work of art. He knew the business. He knew the uses of M1 firestarters. He knew about Pyronol torches and Heat Blocks. He knew about thermite and thermate. He knew about I.M. and P.T. gels, and about phosphorus, red and white. Sometimes he just jiggered fuse boxes, shorting them so cunningly that after they had ignited the building, fire investigators could not tell whether the fire had been accidental or deliberate. Sometimes he used a little white phosphorus, lifting it gently out of its water with long tongs. You had to be careful with that stuff! DeWitt knew people who had used white phosphorus for too many years, who had inhaled too many fumes, and who looked like zombies because there were no bones in their faces anymore.

For 817 East Ninth, DeWitt had selected one of his favorite combinations—sulfuric acid plus a mixture of potassium chlorate and sugar. For good measure, he had brought along a little kerosene. On small fires, where the heat might not be too intense, kerosene was stuff for amateurs, but DeWitt intended to make this a large fire, a very large fire indeed.

DeWitt smiled in the darkness again.

He dropped the cigarette among the broken bricks, leaving it burning, and crossed East Ninth Street to 817, carrying his heavy case. He let himself in with the key he had been given and climbed in his crepe shoes to the fourth floor. There, in an unused janitor's cupboard filled with bottles and boxes, he set the bottom of a plastic-coated milk carton. From a glass vial he poured into this cube several ounces of smoking acid. He checked his watch; he had ten minutes. Around the carton and across the floor, he scattered a white powdery mix. He then backed down the corridor, dousing the cracked old floor with kerosene. He returned to shut the closet door for maximum explosive force, and then descended one floor, to an empty apartment directly underneath. He was gratified to see kerosene already seeping through cracks in the plaster ceiling, dripping to the floor. In a few minutes that ceiling would go up like a bomb.

Here and there, from the light fixture, from the curtain rods, and from the hooks for old swag lamps still in the ceiling, DeWitt began to hang balloons half filled with kerosene. He worked fast. He imagined the acid eating its way through that milk carton.

"Hey! What the hell you doin'?"

DeWitt spun around to face the door. "Acme Exterminators! This building's got . . . Oh. It's *you!*"

Carlos stood in the doorway with his feet apart. There was a bandage across one cheekbone and his lower lip was blue and puffy. He had no weapons. The baseball bat was gone, the axe was gone.

He was not sure why he had come back. Ever since smashing Pa saucer, ever since his encounter with Harry, he had been in turmoil. "What are you *doin'?*" he asked again.

"Doin' my job, kid. 'Scuse me."

"Where *is* everybody?"

DeWitt shook him off. "How should I know? Look, kid, this place is going up in about five minutes. I don't know about you, but I'm . . ."

"You're gonna *torch* it? Kovacs sent you to torch it? He can't do that! This is mine, this place! My *name's* on this place, you understand?"

Scowling, DeWitt tossed the empty kerosene container into his case and slammed the lid. "You had your chance, kid. You blew it. Out of my way. Make way for the big boys."

Carlos hit him.

The blow snapped DeWitt's head against the wall and brought blood spurting from his nose. He rebounded, bashed Carlos with his metal case, and staggered for the stairs. Blood streamed through the fingers pressed to his face. "Gmwout!" he shouted.

Carlos chased him, kicking wildly as the man fled downstairs. "This is *my* building! You go back! Tell Kovacs! Tell Lacey! Whatever happens here I do. Me! Carlos Chavez!"

"Schmoopid!" DeWitt mumbled. "Schmoopid! Domake moise!"

Carlos chased him all the way through the front door, kicking, punching, screaming. Even in the street he was still slashing at the hapless DeWitt when the man dropped his hand from his blood-smeared face and shouted, "What's the *matter* with you? What are you *on?* Lemme go! Get away from here! That place is gonna go up like a Roman candle!"

At that moment, Faye opened the window of her second-floor bedroom and said in a clear, firm mother's voice, "Stop that at once! I won't have you scuffling in the streets. Let go of that man this instant and get in here! Get washed for dinner!"

Carlos froze.

DeWitt gaped in horror.

There she was, framed in candlelight coming from the apartment behind her. She was dressed for some very formal occasion, in a severe, buttoned dress with a floral pattern, a woolly black shawl held in place by a cameo brooch, and a plain black hat with a half veil.

"Young *man,*" she said again, raising her chin, "right *now,* if you please!"

Carlos seized DeWitt's collar. *"You said they were gone! You said they were all out!"*

"I thought they *were!* Let me *go,* man! That building's gonna..."

"No, it's not! It's not! You're gonna go in there and shut it off."

"No way! That building is history. So's everything in it. My job's done, pal! You want to commit suicide, go ahead! Broom closet! Fourth floor!" DeWitt swung his empty steel case hard against the side of Carlos's head and pulled loose. Carlos started after him but then looked back at the frail figure silhouetted in the window, pointing sternly at him. "Young man, right *now!*"

Carlos ran back inside and up to the second floor, taking the steps three at a time. When he burst into the Rileys' apartment, Faye was lighting candles on the table. "That's better," she said. "Wash up, now. Frank'll be home any minute."

In three strides he crossed the room and seized her. "Come on! We're leaving!"

"Leaving? What do you mean, *leaving?*"

He pulled her roughly, and she slapped at his hand, eyes flashing. "Stop that, Bobby! When I tell . . ."

"Lady," Carlos grabbed her shoulders. Sweat streamed off him, staining all the front of his shirt and plastering his hair to his head. "I'm not . . ." An idea hit him. He controlled his panic. He smiled sweetly. "Gee, Mom," he said, "I'm sorry. I just wanted to show you something."

"Show me . . .? What?"

"My . . . my . . . car. Yeah, gee, don't you remember the new car?"

Faye stepped back. Something was suddenly wrong. Very wrong.

"What car?"

Carlos pulled her towards the door. *"My* car. Right? Here we go! Don't wanna be late for the game! Dad's waiting downstairs, and you know how he is!"

Faye stopped. "Your father? *Waiting?*"

"Yeah, good old Dad. What a guy . . ." He tugged on her arm, but she yanked it away, shrinking back. Both hands went to her mouth. Her eyes widened. Her whole world tipped crazily and spun away, leaving only a strange young man gripping her arm.

"You're not him!"

"Mother, please . . ." Carlos reached for her with his other hand, but she pulled free.

"You're not Bobby!" She turned and ran into the bedroom.

Carlos lunged, but she had already slammed the door and locked it. "Oh, God, lady! Don't wake up *now!* Goddammit! *There isn't time for this!*" He kicked the door hard; it stayed shut.

Wide-eyed, he backed toward the entrance. "Broom closet," he muttered. "Fourth floor!"

He dashed for the stairs.

But time had run out. On the counter of the dark closet two storys above, the first trickle of sulfuric acid ate through the plasticized container and seeped, smoking, towards the potassium chlorate. Just as Carlos grabbed the door, the two substances combined—and ignited.

The closet detonated. Turning from the flash, Carlos flung himself to the floor as a claw of flame snatched at him, blistering the opposite wall of the hallway. Acid, kerosene, old cleaning solvents, fracturing gas lines—all fed an instant inferno that sucked a whirlwind of oxygen up the stairwell and blew out the ceiling and the wall. Covered with dust and debris, scorched and scraped, Carlos struggled up and away, lurching for the stairs just as the kerosene-soaked floor collapsed, bursting the balloons DeWitt had hung beneath. Flaming kerosene spewed in all directions. Carlos reeled away from this inferno, choking and gagging, and somehow got back to the second floor.

The door of the Rileys' apartment was still open, but the hallway was already clogged with smoke. Flames danced through cracks in the ceiling and licked down the walls. Carlos lurched in, half crawling under the pall, but Faye was gone. Not in the living room. Not in the bedroom. In the kitchen he grabbed a dish towel and drenched it, clamping it over his mouth and nose. He drew one, two deep breaths through this filter and then lowered it to shout, "Mrs. Riley! *Where are you!* We gotta get outta here!"

Her voice came back very calm and very firm, echoing. "I'm not leaving!"

The bathroom! Carlos hurled himself at the locked door, and it splintered open. Smoke billowed in behind him. She was standing in the bathtub, perfectly dignified and dressed as he had left her, in her shawl and her veiled hat, holding to her breast the albums with all the photographs of other years, all the photographs of Bobby. "Young man," she said, "I'll tell you once more, I have no intention . . ."

Carlos grabbed her. He yanked down the shower curtain, swept her up in it, and threw her over his shoulder, losing his wet towel in the process. When he staggered back into the apartment, he couldn't see and he couldn't breathe. The doorway had already turned into a wall of flame. He lunged for the window and kicked. The glass burst and the curtains flung themselves through in the hot wind, flapping like the arms of a trapped and desperate creature.

Carlos was engulfed in smoke and flame. It seemed to him then that he became something other than himself, because he was watching himself, a man bearing something precious, surrounded by a chaos of raging smoke and toppling, flaming debris, helplessly sinking as he crawled toward a tiny light at the end of a tunnel that got longer and longer, blacker and blacker.

Tiny and very far away, Carlos heard sirens.

The cab carrying Harry back from the hospital had to pull into the curb to let fire trucks rush by.

Harry didn't notice, at first. He was thinking about

Marisa and about the fact that the baby still had not arrived before Mason had come out and told him, "Harry, the doctor says it'll be a while. Maybe you should go back. In case there's more trouble, you know?"

He had nodded and gone out and found a cab, but he kept looking back through the rear window, thinking about Marisa, wondering if she and the baby were all right. Harry knew very little about the arrival of babies; he knew that they needed a lot of hot water, because he had seen doctors calling for it in old movies.

And so, he worried. Suddenly the cabbie was saying, *"What's that? There!"* Peering through the windshield Harry saw smoke billowing, and a glow on the mirrored fronts of new office towers. People were running.

"Don't think I can get any closer," the cabbie said. "Looks like we got a little problem . . ."

But already Harry was thrusting a bill at him, climbing out of the car, beginning to run, his horrified gaze fixed on 817 East Ninth Street—home.

The building was an inferno. Most of the windows had blown out and flames were licking up the outside of the brick walls. As Harry arrived, the roof collapsed and the chimney toppled inwards, sending a roaring volcano of sparks hundreds of feet into the air.

And there was Frank. White, wide-eyed, gaping in horror, he pushed his way through the crowd towards Harry, saying his wife's name as if it were a question—"Faye? Faye? *Faye?*" Clenched in his right hand was what looked to Harry like a bundle of sticks, but which, as Frank drew closer, became three crushed cigars, sticking at crazy angles through his fingers.

He lurched forward, tripping over a hose that two firemen were hauling off a pumper. Several other hoses were already in action, sending futile streams arcing up and into the hulk of the building, to be vaporized instantly in the tremendous heat. "Back!" one of the firemen shouted at Frank. "Out of the way!" And he pushed him hard enough to send him reeling into the crowd.

But Harry was moving, too. Harry was moving right through the firemen and police, moving with a boxer's deft steps across the tangle of hoses and debris towards the east side of the building, where the wall was still sufficiently intact to give some protection against the heat, and where something was lying on the fire escape, something that looked like a man facedown with a bundle of rags on his back. Harry was headed straight for that place, not fast but inexorably, ignoring the shouts and curses that followed him, brushing off a helmeted policeman who lunged at him.

The wall was too hot to touch. Bricks and chunks of masonry toppled off and crashed to the ground, clanging on the fire escape. That rickety structure had pulled loose and was swaying; in fact, the top had already folded over like a strand of limp licorice.

Harry climbed. In seconds he had reached the two unconscious forms on the second-storey landing. He draped Faye over his shoulder, hooked his arm under Carlos's, and grabbed his shirt front. Then down he went, backwards, Carlos's heels bumping on every step.

Helpers waited at the bottom. Sturdy, shouting firemen seized the three of them and half dragged, half carried them across the vacant lot and through the police cordon, to waiting ambulances.

The east wall, fire escape and all, collapsed inwards with a crash that shook the earth beneath them.

Medics cut away the shower curtain that Carlos had wrapped around Faye. It had protected her from cuts and burns, but not from smoke. She was gray and limp. Trembling, Frank seized her hands and raised them to his face.

They felt cold. One of the medics felt for a pulse and nodded. Another fitted an oxygen mask over her face. "You her husband?"

Frank nodded.

"Let's go!" He helped Frank up into the ambulance, up beside the stretcher. The doors slammed. The siren whined.

Medics loaded Carlos onto another stretcher, giving him oxygen as they did so, and whisked him into a second ambulance. He was bruised and cut, and his left arm was broken or dislocated, sticking out at an unnatural angle, but he was alive. From the edge of the crowd two of his old gang members, Poncho and Ramirez, solemnly watched him pass. "Just so you know," Ramirez said, touching one of the cops on the arm, "that guy's a hero. He don't even *live* in that building."

Medics started to lead Harry to yet another ambulance, but the big man drew back. "Come on down to the hospital," they said. "Get checked over."

Harry shook his head.

"You might feel okay now, but there'll be some shock."

Again Harry shook his head. "I'm okay," he said. "I'm gonna stay."

The medics shrugged. "Suit yourself. You live here?"

"I did," Harry said. He turned to look. The building was just a blazing pile of rubble now. Streams from two hoses still played across it, but the others had turned their attention to cooling the trailers on the construction sites. On the far side of the site, the white sign advertising Lacey Plaza rose above the chaos: ELEGANCE, CONVENIENCE, SECURITY.

14 _____

MIRACULOUSLY, THE FRONT of the cafe survived. There was nothing behind, or above, or on either side, except the concrete steps of what had been 817 East Ninth, leading nowhere.

But the old wooden facade survived. It was charred black, its doorless entrance gaped like a dead mouth, its windows were smashed, its awning was shredded to rags. Water dripped from its ruined moldings into the rubble, gurgling away with drainage from the rest of the ruin.

Everything smelled like an old, wet campfire.

Sitting on the steps in the gray dawn, Harry decided that was exactly what it smelled like, like the sodden campfire when he had been taken on a cub scout trip at the age of eight, and it had rained all night. His leaders had tried to cook breakfast in the rain, on a smoldering roll of toilet paper.

"So," he said to the mongrel beside him. "What are *you* gonna do?"

The dog gazed at Harry with doleful eyes. His head lay on his paws. His tail swatted the wet concrete once, twice.

"You got a home around here? Huh?" Harry thought he recognized the dog as the first of the throng that had followed him the previous night. He thought he remembered those droopy ears, that straggly hair on his muzzle that drooped like a Zapata moustache. But he could not remember when the dog had joined him on the steps. Sometime during the night he must have crept close and lain down beside him. "Better go home." Harry said, rubbing the dog's ears. "Get warm. Have breakfast."

The dog lay still, glancing up at Harry, waiting.

Around 7:30, pickup trucks began to arrive at the construction site, and doors slammed shut. Harry could hear low whistles and exclamations of astonishment from the workers. For ten or fifteen minutes they drifted over in little groups to stand with their hands on their hips, to stare at the wreck of the building, to stare at Harry.

Harry and the dog stared back. Once the dog growled low in his throat, but Harry rubbed his ears again and said, "It doesn't matter. It doesn't matter anymore."

Soon the heavy machinery started up for the day's work, and shortly before eight, Gus, the driver of Chief Broom, detached his thunderous machine from the others and headed towards the ruin of Rileys' Cafe.

"Cleanup time," Harry said softly to the dog, watching him come.

The police had cordoned off the ruin with a length of yellow tape, strung on stakes set in little cairns of rubble. When he reached this ribbon, Gus stopped the machine, and for a moment the man on the steps and the man on the bulldozer stared at each other across the immense, shuddering blade. Then slowly, Gus lifted off his hard hat in a small salute that Harry acknowledged with a motion of the hand that hung between his knees.

Gus shifted into neutral and climbed down, letting the machine idle. He came forward to the tape.

"Got orders to smooth this out," Gus said, making a flat gesture.

Harry nodded. "Yeah."

"Think I can do that pretty soon?"

"Nope," Harry said. "Don't think so."

"Gonna be there awhile, huh?"

Harry nodded.

"Waitin' for a miracle, maybe?"

"Maybe," Harry said, still nodding.

Kovacs arrived then. Kovacs arrived in his black limousine wearing a crisp blue suit, looking satisfied. He got out of his car. "Well," he said to Gus, waving, "get on with it! Finish it off!"

Gus pointed at Harry and the dog on the steps.

"Get him out of the way! Call the cops if you have to. He's trespassing!"

"No, sir."

"What?"

Gus sighed. "You won, Kovacs. You won. So what's your hurry now? Why not let the guy sit for a while if he wants to?"

"Because I want this job *finished*, that's why. Now get on with it!"

Gus shook his head again. "When he moves, we move."

"Are you refusing an order?"

Gus spat. "I don't take orders from you, Mr. Kovacs. I take orders from Sammy the foreman. He's right over there, if you want to see him. He's the guy in the white hat." He climbed back into the seat of Chief Broom and rammed the machine into reverse. "I'm backing up now," he shouted as he revved the diesel. "You better tell your driver to move that car."

Kovacs scurried back to the limo, shouting something that could not be heard above the roar of the machine.

So Harry stayed, and the dog stayed with him. Sometimes he scratched the dog's ears. "What are *you* waitin' for? Don't you have anyplace to go either? Huh?"

The dog rested his head sometimes on his paws, sometimes on Harry's knees.

Harry worried about Marisa. He worried about the baby; something *must* be wrong or Mason would have come back by now. He worried about Faye. He remembered how limp and light she had been on his shoulder, and he remembered too the awful sight of her head on the pillow of the stretcher, the respirator clamped over her nose and mouth, her face almost as white as her hair...

He should go to the hospital. He should go to see her. But he couldn't leave the building. It was absurd to stay, really, because there *was* no building anymore. It was a heap of trash. His room was just a hole full of debris and scummy water.

But he still felt as if he lived there. After all those years it was hard not to feel about 817 East Ninth as he had felt that first night when the residents had brought him in and made a home for him in the basement when he had nowhere else to go. The Rileys had done that, and the Hogensons, and the Grandeys, and the Moscowitzes. They had all helped him. And they all kept passing now in front of Harry's eyes as they used to be, smiling and laughing, and clapping him on the back, and going down to the cafe for supper in the evening. He kept seeing the building as it had been then, all glowing with its windows open on a summer evening and kids running past, and people calling to one another, and Artie Shaw's sweet clarinet sounds drifting out of the cafe, under the green awning.

Also, he had hope. It was absurd, but as the shadows lengthened and lights began to flick on in the shadowy corners of the city, Harry knew he had hope. He did not know what he had hope *in*. He had no reason for hope. He had lost everything. He didn't even have a bed to sleep in that night, or enough money to buy a cup of coffee. But there it was: he hoped. He could *feel* it, like a huge flower blossoming inside him, or like a big soft light glowing out of him, into space.

He knew that if he believed strongly enough, if he waited long enough, something would happen.

That was why when Gus leaned through the window of his truck on his way home and asked, "Hey, fella, howsabout comin' with me?" Harry shook his head.

"Appreciate it," he said. "But no thanks."

"Still waitin' for that miracle, huh?"

"That's right," Harry said. "That's what I'm waitin' for."

All that day, all that night, Faye lay in her hospital bed, staring blankly at the wall. Frank sat beside her, smoothing her hair, clasping her hands in both of his, talking earnestly to her. He told her that he wanted her to get better soon, because they were going to take a trip together. They were going to take that holiday they had talked about for so long—maybe to Asbury Park, maybe to Atlantic City, maybe even to the Grand Canyon. He told her that he thought he might even retire now, that he had worked long enough, and he tried hard to keep from his voice the quaver that slipped in whenever he remembered his beloved cafe clenched in great claws of flame.

He told her that he loved her; many times he told her that he loved her.

He stayed with her until at last the doctor came in and insisted that he go to the cafeteria for something to eat. In the hall he put his arm around Frank's shoulders. "Physically, Mr. Riley, your wife is fine. She's bruised and stiff from what happened to her. The smoke inhalation won't leave any lasting effects. I want to keep her for a day or two, just for observation, but the problem isn't physical, so far as I can tell."

"Will she . . . come out of it?"

"You mean will she recognize you again? Recognize her surroundings? I don't know. She's had a profound shock that could aggravate her condition. We'll have to see, Mr. Riley. We'll just have to wait and see."

But she did not recognize Frank all that afternoon, and she did not recognize Mason when he came down from the maternity ward with news: "A girl! Isn't that wonderful! Six pounds five ounces! She's beautiful! Wait till you see her! She's just like her mother, only wizened up, kind of, with little fists, like this," and Mason did a fair imitation of a grimacing, very healthy newborn child.

But although Frank had laughed at this news and wrung Mason's hand, Faye gave no indication of having heard. She lay with her face turned away from them, towards the window. Yet, she was not looking at the window, or at the sky beyond. She was not looking at anything.

"I'll be back later," Mason said quietly. Then, seeing Frank's haggard expression, he said, "You better get some rest. You better go ho—"

"Yeah," Frank said, nodding bitterly. "Exactly. Where's home now?"

For the rest of the afternoon and into the dusk, Frank sat

holding his wife's hands and talking to her, talking to her as if just by doing that he could bring her back from the lonely, empty place where she had gone, the blank place, the place where there were no realities at all.

In the deepening shadows, he took his glasses off to dry his eyes with his handkerchief, and while he was doing that, the door opened again, and he turned, his blurred vision playing tricks in the near darkness, to see a young man silhouetted in the light from the hall.

"It's me, Mr. Riley. Carlos."

Frank found his glasses and the light switch. "Oh, Carlos. Come in."

One arm hung in a sling. In the other Carlos held a bouquet of little flowers. "I . . . I brought these for Mrs. Riley. They're pansies, lady said."

Frank took them out of the bandaged hand, nodding.

"And I wanna say I'm sorry. I wanna tell you that. If I'd thought . . ."

But Frank waved him to silence. "It doesn't matter now, Carlos. None of that matters. You saved her. You brought her back to me."

Carlos came close and stared at Faye's expressionless face, looked into her unseeing eyes. He shook his head slowly. "I dunno, Mr. Riley." He gestured with his good hand, and the bandages wrapping the burns made it look like a white bird flying into darkness.

"Wait a minute! Maybe . . . Come over here, Carlos. I just wanna try . . . Faye? Faye, honey, look who's come to see you! *Bobby's here!*"

Faye blinked. Very slowly she turned her face from the wall. She looked at her husband with a clear and level gaze. She looked at Carlos.

And then, softly, Faye Riley wept.

* * *

Alone with the small dog, Harry waited for the miracle. Perhaps because he had hope, that was why—when the last of the workmen had closed the trailers and shut off the machines, when night had fallen and the traffic sounds had hushed as if the great city itself had heard something inexplicable and was listening—perhaps that was why the miracle occurred.

The dog knew it first. He began to whimper, as if welcoming his master home at the end of a long day. His tail slapped wildly on the wet concrete.

"Hey," Harry said. "Buddy. Whatsa..."

And then he heard what the dog heard—a high-pitched whine getting louder fast, not a siren, not an aircraft—something coming at high speed from the south.

Harry stood up slowly, breaking into an incredulous smile. He spread his arms in welcome. The next moment a small flying object hurtled past at such speed that Harry scarcely had time to recognize him before he was banking around and coming back to bound into Harry's pocket.

"Weems!"

The little saucer leapt out and onto Harry's palm, beeping wildly.

"Hey!" Harry said. "Great to see ya, buddy! Great to see *all* of you!" Flotsam and Jetsam zoomed in, hovering a moment with the pale light from their eyes glowing on Harry's face, before zipping into the demolished vestibule.

"Aw," Harry said sadly, "it's a beautiful thought. It really is. But you guys can't be serious. Not the whole building! Why, to do that you'd need..."

Suddenly the night filled with resonance, a deep, throbbing stately thrumming that sounded at first like a train approaching from a long way off, and then like many,

many trains, and then like nothing Harry Noble had ever heard before, like nothing on earth.

". . . a whole army, a whole army of . . ."

He turned slowly, knowing what he would see.

Ma and Pa came first. Behind them, lights glowing like a suspended city, came hundreds of saucers, thousands, all shapes, all sizes, all ready to work.

". . . fixers," Harry Noble said.

Majestically, like robed arms, the wings of the saucer flotilla swung forward and enclosed the rubble heaps and the empty place where the old building, loved by all its tenants, had once stood so proudly.

At dawn Faye Riley sat up in her hospital bed and said, "I want to go home."

Frank snapped awake.

He fumbled for his glasses.

He had fallen asleep in the chair beside her bed. The last things he remembered were the dull glow of the night-light and the many hospital sounds—doctors being paged, and carts rattling past the doorway, and footfalls of hurrying nurses. But now, suddenly, there was the sun blazing in at him! And there was his wife's sensible voice saying again, "Did you hear me, Frank? Let's go home."

"Faye," he said, gaping. "You're . . ."

"I'm all right. I'm fine. And I want to get out of this place."

"Sure, honey, but . . ."

"No buts." She swung her legs over the side of the bed. "Do you see what time it is? If we don't go now, we won't have the cafe open for breakfast."

"The cafe!" He didn't know where to begin.

She turned towards him.

She looked serene and very beautiful. The color had

come back to her cheeks, and her eyes were clear. "I had a bad dream," she said. She reached out and took her husband's face between her hands, and kissed him.

"We're going home," she said, smiling radiantly to someone over Frank's shoulder. "You've brought my clothes?"

Two young policemen were standing in the doorway, their caps under their arms. One of them was carrying a small, old-fashioned suitcase. They both looked wide-eyed and wary. "The big guy asked us to bring this to you. He said you'd need it."

"Harry?"

"Harry, yeah."

"Bless his heart! How thoughtful! Would you boys mind just waiting in the hall while I get dressed? I'll be right along."

Frank went out into the hall with them.

"She knows," one of the young cops said.

"Knows? Knows what?" Frank asked him.

They looked at each other. The one who had been silent pointed very slowly and deliberately at the closed door of the hospital room and then at Frank, as if he wanted to get something quite straight. *"She* knows, and *you* don't."

"Knows *what?"*

The policeman exhaled softly, puffing out his cheeks as he did so. The other shook his head. "You wouldn't believe us if we told you, Mr. Riley. Best thing is just for us to take you down there and show you. Even then you might not believe it."

The door swung open. "Ready!" Faye said.

Mason Baylor was already in the squad car, waiting for them. He shrugged when Frank asked, "What *is* this?"

"There'll be a lot of people," Faye said, climbing into

the back seat between the two men. "A *lot* of people. We'll have a busy morning in the cafe. No helpers, either. How about you, Mason? Could you help us out for a while?"

Mason looked at Frank. He looked at the palms of his hands, spread between his knees. "Mrs. Riley . . . I want to help you. I *do*. I *will* help you. But I gotta tell you that the cafe, the whole building . . ."

The police car rounded a corner.

There stood the building, 817 East Ninth Street.

It gleamed in the rising sun.

Its bricks were warm and red, as if freshly baked and newly mortared, free of the grime of the years. New black paint glinted on the fire escape, and the window frames and crenellations glowed in rich brown. Sunlight flashed on polished window panes. In the southwest corner, Rileys' Cafe was fully restored, pristine again with its wooden facade, and gold-lettered windows, and green awning with FINE FOOD on the scalloped border. Above, blazing in the corner of the building, was the wonderful neon that Faye remembered from the fifties, RILEYS' CAFE.

The building was new again.

"You see?" Faye said. "There are people waiting already."

Indeed there were.

The street was blocked with people. They spilled off the sidewalk, pointing and gawking. Lights flashing, siren purring, the cruiser inched through the crowds and stopped in front of 817 East Ninth. Two other units had arrived before them, and officers had begun to clear the street, moving people back onto the sidewalks. Officials from the Fire Department stood staring beside their red van, hands on hips. And Lacey's black limousine was parked right at the entrance, with two burly gentlemen in sunglasses and gray chauffeurs' uniforms guarding it. A television truck stood with its doors flung open while the crew readied their camera and sound gear, and while a young interviewer fixed her hair in front of a mirror in the cab. Hurrying past, checking his tape recorder, a reporter stopped when some- one on the street grabbed his arm and pointed into the rear seat of the cruiser. He came back to the car.

"You Mr. and Mrs. Riley? You the folks who live here? Own the cafe?"

Frank nodded, helping Faye out of the car. He was gap- ing at the building. Faye stood for a minute without an- swering, radiant in the sunshine, surveying every crisp and beautiful detail of Rileys' Cafe. At last she said, "We are."

The man pushed close with his microphone. "Mrs. Riley, twenty-four hours ago this building was burned to the ground. It was a heap of rubble. There was nothing left of the original structure except . . ."

"Why don't you come inside and have coffee, dear? We're going to open up now, aren't we, Frank?"

"But, Mrs. Riley, just one question, please, while I have you here. Are you responsible for this?"

She laughed happily. "Certainly not."

"But how . . . how did you people . . ."

She leaned close, whispering to him, pushing the mi- crophone away gently with the back of her hand. "With a little help from our *friends*," she whispered. "Nobody, ever, does anything alone."

Other people crowded in, among them the TV crew jos- tling for pictures and sound. "Mr. Riley . . . Mr. Riley . . ."

But Frank paid no attention. He was seeing only Harry, Harry pushing through the crowd, delirious with joy, his fists lifted high in triumph. When he reached Frank and Faye, he hugged them so hard that he lifted them together off their feet. "You shoulda seen 'em!" he said. "There was hundreds of 'em. Hundreds and *hundreds* of 'em."

Microphones pushed close. "Hundreds of what?" somebody asked.

On the edge of the crowd, a small dog was running in ecstatic circles around Mason, leaping up to lick his hand. Absentmindedly he patted it, wandering across towards the entrance to his apartment. He had almost reached the steps when he heard his name being called.

"Do you remember me, Mr. Baylor? Alma Thompson from the Historical Landmarks Commission? I just want to tell you that I *love* it! I *love* what you've done. I don't know *how* you've done it—it's nothing short of a miracle, if you ask me—but it's perfect. Perfect! Exactly in period. And I want you to know that we shall be designating it immediately. It will be protected just as it is!"

"We can go on living here?"

"Oh, yes. Of course. You just won't be able to change anything, that's all. At least, anything on the outside."

"Ms. Thompson," Mason laughed. "We don't *want* to change anything."

"Well, of course you don't!" She laughed. "Of course, there'll have to be a plaque. Probably there, beside the door." She pointed.

At that moment, Martin Lacey emerged from the building. He strode towards the limousine, with Kovacs hurrying along beside him.

". . . prefab of some sort," Kovacs was saying. His eyes were glazed, his face twitching. He was sweating heavily. "It can't be real, know what I mean, Mr. Lacey? Not *really* real. It's some kind of trick. Some kind of optical . . . a hologram, maybe!"

Lacey smiled stiffly at the TV crew hurrying towards them. "Kovacs," he said, "you're fired."

And then the reporters surrounded him, and the two

stocky men in chauffeurs' uniforms were shouldering them back, clearing a path to the limousine.

The young woman with the microphone said, "Mr. Lacey, this building was reported burned to the ground last night. Is that true? Can you give us an explanation?"

"Looks like somebody made a mistake," Lacey said, laughing softly. "Excuse me, please."

"Well, what are your plans for this site, in view of what has happened?"

"My plans remain unchanged."

"Are you aware that the Historical Landmarks Commission plans to designate this site, protecting it against demolition? Do you have anything to say about that?"

"No," Lacey said. "Nothing." And he bent down and vanished behind the smoked glass of the car. The door clicked shut.

As the limousine drove away, the reporters hurried over to the front of the cafe, where Frank Riley was opening his door. He fitted a brass key into the shiny brass lock. Through the beveled glass of the door, through the large windows with the gilt lettering, past the potted plants and the crisp lace curtains, the crowd could see the cool and shadowy interior of the cafe. They could see the soda fountain; they could see the clean little tables, waiting.

"Open in ten minutes!" Frank said, smiling broadly. "And this morning the coffee's on the house!"

Inside, in the silence and the coolness, Faye and Frank had a moment alone together. They held hands, like kids going into a strange and wonderful place, and now as they gazed at what they had been given, their arms went around each other.

"Oh, Frank! It's just like it used to be when we were . . ."

"Young," Frank said softly. And for that magical moment they *were* young, and it *was* 1946, and the war was over and all their lives lay ahead of them, lives that would be spent here, with customers who would become old friends, and with neighbors like the Hogensons who would become part of their family.

And with Bobby. Bobby. . .

It was only a moment in human time, a moment during which two old people stood holding each other in the dappled sunlight of an old cafe, sharing the same memories, seeing the same faces, hearing the same laughter and the same ghostly melodies drifting out of the old nickelodeon. It was only a moment, yet it seemed to both of them that it might go on forever. Perhaps, in other dimensions that they could never fully understand, it *did*.

And then reality returned. Mason and Harry came in through the apartment vestibule, past the policeman stationed there to keep strangers out, and down the corridor to the doorway of the cafe, so full of wonder at what they were seeing that they could not speak. They could only laugh incredulously, Mason with his hands spread, shaking his head, Harry slamming the fist of one big hand into the other, again and again.

Carlos's face appeared at the side window, hands shading his eyes, and Frank signaled him towards the front door, and patted him on the shoulder as he entered with his bandaged hand awkward in front of him. "Come on in here, son. We need your help."

"Carlos," Faye said, taking his hand in both of hers.

They all went up to the roof together, passing on their way the opened doors of apartments beautifully restored, and up a stairway that smelled of fresh plaster and fresh paint, and out into the sunlight of a graveled roof free of the grime of decades. The little roof garden was just as it had been, with its chairs arranged in a decorous circle around the table, under the crisp umbrella. All the Christmas lights glowed in new sockets, attached to a thick, new, heavy-duty cord. But the plug on the end of that cord no longer led into the pigeon coop. In fact, there was no pigeon coop anymore. Nor was there any pile of scrap metal, or anything else to suggest that the saucers had ever been there.

The five of them stood a moment, looking wistfully at the place where the pigeon coop had been.

"W: didn't even thank them," Frank said.

Faye smiled. "There are lots of ways of thanking them. You know that. You don't have to *say* it."

"The great thing is," Mason said, "they came once, they can come again, if we need them enough."

"No," Faye shook her head firmly. "They won't be back. How many miracles do you want? No, it's up to us, now. We're gonna make our *own* miracles. So let's get started. There're a lot of hungry people downstairs."

At that moment, there came a little whining sound, a little fluttering that caused them all to turn south toward the sound, where two bright lights approached rapidly, just above the roofs. But it was not a saucer. It was a television helicopter. It circled and then swept in low, with the cameraman, secure in his belts, leaning through the open door.

"Wave, everybody!" Faye said. "Wave! The world is watching!"

And so it was that Marisa, nursing her baby, saw them all on the news at noon, from her room in the hospital. There they were—Faye and Frank, and Carlos and Harry, and Mason. Her Mason. There they were, waving their arms joyfully from the roof of what appeared to be (if you didn't know the story) an ordinary old-style apartment building with a little restaurant in the corner of its bottom floor, as the helicopter circled and the announcer said something about a major development having been brought to a standstill by a small but determined group of residents.

"See?" Marisa said to her baby. "There's where we're going! There's home!"

Imagine them now. At home.

Imagine Harry in a bright workshop beside the furnace room, clad in special coveralls bearing the crest of the Historical Landmarks Commission. Imagine him going on his rounds with a small dog, maintaining every detail of 817 East Ninth in mint condition. Imagine Marisa posing for Mason's paintings, taking her child every day up to the roof where a real garden of potted flowers and trees flourishes. Imagine Carlos, crisp in tie and jacket, showing diners to tables in Rileys' Cafe, and Gus, bringing his grandson in for his first soda, and the Hogensons driving in from the Island Manor Retirement Village. Imagine Sid sipping coffee in the evening, listening to Benny Goodman, saying, "Muriel, about that apartment upstairs. Maybe we just oughta take it . . ."

Best of all, imagine Faye and Frank, alone at the end of a long and tiring day, closing the cafe, turning the lights down low, dropping a nickel into the old machine, and dancing in each other's arms to the soft strains of "Moonlight Serenade," their eyes closed.

Imagine how the old building appears now from some point high, high above the city—a community, sailing on through time like a great, well-lighted ship . . .